D[O N'T]
F [BLEEP] K
WITH THE
COLOUREDS

ANDRE DUZA

deadite
press

deadite
press

DEADITE PRESS
P.O. BOX 10065
PORTLAND, OR 97296
www.DEADITEPRESS.com

AN ERASERHEAD PRESS COMPANY
www.ERASERHEADPRESS.com

ISBN: 978-1-62105-307-1

Don't F[Bleep]K with
the Coloureds
—5—

Retrograde
—57—

Night of the Day of the
Celebrated Folks
—101—

DON'T F [BLEEP] K WITH THE COLOUREDS

WITH THE

COLOUREDS

FADE IN:

White letters against a black screen:
Generic Films Presents…

DISSOLVE TO:

It is the middle of the night. We open on a wide, three-story, Rundbogenstil-style building set dead center in the frame. The letters carved into the archway above the large front door read: **Harrington House Retirement Center.**

Narrator: Someone is killing the residents of Harrington House...

CUT TO:

A hand wrapped in a latex surgical glove fills the frame, fingers tense and straight. A second hand simultaneously pulls the glove at the wrist to work the fingers in.

Narrator: …someone who promised to care for them.

CUT TO:

A nervous-looking woman dressed in office attire is talking on the phone. Fear colors her voice.

Nervous-looking woman: I think Dr. Everhardt is experimenting on the residents. She is suddenly startled by someone who enters the room from behind. She turns and sees a distinguished-looking, middle-aged man (Dr. Everhardt) standing there.

CUT TO:

A group of nurses struggle to hold down an elderly man who thrashes in pain on his hospital bed. Heart monitors are beeping. The nurses are talking over each other. The man's eyes are rolled back, veins bulging. His body shoots to a rigid arch as the worst pain hits him. He is foaming at the mouth and shaking his head back and forth in a vain attempt to signal "no." His screams begin to echo.

Narrator: Lifetime Movie Channel presents a film based on a true story. Crystal Bernard, Tracey Gold, and Bruce Boxleitner star in...

There is a sudden distortion.

The narrator's voice recedes to incoherent mumbling. The frame begins to stutter and tear, then finally melt as if the film is burning.

Beneath the celluloid surface, words began to materialize...

Three years ago...

The winding driveway that led up the hill to the wide, three-story, Rundbogenstil-style building (the Harrington House Retirement Center) writhed with activity like a tongue rolling out in effigy of something dead sexy. Sirens screeching like mechanized infant calls, amplified by the dark-matter din of night in the 'burbs. Two police cars raced up the long driveway, which was finger-flecked by branches that reached out on both sides from the semi-wooded land between Route 1 below and the old building at the top of the hill. "Private Property, No Trespass" signs dotted the road.

The first two officers at the scene (McMahon and Shields) were already crouching behind their opened car doors when the first backup car roared up, slid sideways, and stopped a few feet from them. Then the next ones screeched to a halt right up on them.

Officer McMahon waved his hand down to signal Officers three (Simmons), four (Tate), five (Carter), and six (Reilly) to stay the fuck down. The new arrivals crouched in the open night and assumed defensive positions behind their cars' bulk.

"So, what've we got?" Reilly inquired, hungry for action.

This was Cloverleaf County after all. The most that ever happened here was the occasional date rape on campus at the college or a drunken bar fight over a chick between privileged frat boys.

"Nothing yet," McMahon responded. "A neighbor phoned in the complaint. Said she heard gunshots while she was out walking her dog."

"Spotted some movement in one of the upstairs windows," said Shields, pointing with his eyes. "Not sure if it's our shooter."

Sporting a knowing grimace, Simmons grumbled, "Nearest house is half a mile from here. What the hell's she doing walking her dog in front of this place?"

"Looking for trouble... just like everyone else," Shields responded.

"It was a rhetorical question, man. Of course she was looking for trouble."

It wasn't the first time the police had been called to Harrington House. In fact, they'd been around more than they would have liked lately. The old folks had been acting strange lately, running around naked, scaring the locals, and playing mean-spirited pranks on each other and the staff.

Harrington House was a place for well-to-do retirees. The brochure boasted grand ballrooms and suites sporting décor and furnishings from the 1920s and '30s. "Take a trip back to the good old days," the pamphlet claimed, "to a time when gentility reigned, when women were ladies and men were gentlemen." Elegant social gatherings and theme parties in the style of old Hollywood were touted as the norm.

"So, what's it gonna be this time?" said McMahon. "Some old fart who forgot to take his medicine?"

"An old fart with a gun," Shields added.

McMahon rolled his eyes.

"You have a knack for pointing out the obvious, Shields..."

Though generally an overlooked sound, the click of a heavy lock sliding open screamed at them from the front door. Bouncing to ready, the officers trained their guns on the sound, following its echo back from the air around them to the front door as it yawned open and allowed a woman to exit before slamming shut.

Her hips spoke loudly through the thigh-length

nurse's uniform that stuck to her ample curves like white on rice. A Harrington House crest was stitched just above her right breast. Her intoxicated state fell upon them secondary to her overall beauty. In fact, it wasn't until she nearly fell down the front steps that they noticed her inebriation.

It was a miracle that she didn't fall on her face. The move that she performed to save her balance, like a retarded step and slide, was the kind of thing that she could have never duplicated no matter how hard she tried.

"Are you all right, ma'am?" McMahon called out, sympathetic, yet stern. "Is there anyone else inside?"

Judging by the look in her eyes, she was somewhere else entirely (and ridin' bareback on some quality shit).

The police, with their little guns and flashing lights, were nothing to the toxic god who violated her sobriety. To her impaired eyes, they were like gnats bouncing around the beacon of the red and blue orbs, swirling and stuttering, making colorful tracers.

"I said, is there anyone else inside?"

—

Lulled into calm by her drunkenness, the officers relaxed their gun-arms, hands loosening their grips. They traded faces to decide who'd approach her. None of them wanted to come off as overeager, even though they all felt the same tingle in their loins. As indirect an opportunity as it might have been, it was still an opportunity to secure some down-the-road-pussy once this chick was all rehabbed and back in the world.

The way she began to move her hips sparked a lurid curiosity in them, well, five of them anyway. Married with children, Officer Jack Tate was as straight as they come. He had even convinced himself that looking at other women that way was a sin.

The others did everything to get a good look at what was about to happen. Fuck safety.

The nurse writhed as they watched, their expressions adopting a figurative dog-pant, their eyes bulging like the fronts of their trousers in testament to dirty, stinkin' sex vibes.

Hanging onto visions of hinted-at nakedness that enhanced the scene, they gawked like prepubescent boys who were tasting real lust for the first time as the nurse let her uniform fall from her shoulders. It caught and lingered at each curve of her S dance before eventually landing in a soft heap around her dainty feet.

Disbelief made the officers smile at the extended full-frontal shot that she gave them.

Tate, who pitied her behavior, shook his head.

The woman's body was firm; her torso long with subtle curves; her skin glowing sepia, with licks of dark brown around her plump nipples and radiating from her wide eyes. They seemed to shine brighter now that she was naked. The look on her face said "I'm high as fuck," yet behind it was solid confidence.

Tate's first plan–to simply clear his throat–didn't even come close to diverting his colleagues attention away from the naked, writhing woman.

Plan number two–grabbing a blanket from his squad car and approaching her with it held out in front of him–only made the other officers groan, as if he was killing their buzz.

But then…

They didn't notice it all at once, but they all eventually saw it: the impression of subdermal arms and hands caressing and embracing the nurse and causing her to sway euphorically to their slithering embraces.

Tate, who was the closest to her, was the first to see it. He didn't want to touch her from the get-go, mainly out of disgust and some twisted idea of loyalty to his wife, but now he was plain-old scared. They all were. One or two of the men hinted at raising their weapons.

The rhythm of her dance suggested a slow, seductive, yet animalistic melody; the skin-deep appendages proffered eerie strings.

The woman turned her back to them and jutted her tight, round ass outward. The dark valley between well-rounded teardrops of flesh invited ogling eyes to look closer. Subdermal hands teased the teardrops open and let them bounce closed.

———

When she turned back around, a single blue eye, reddened by anger or maybe hatred, glared at the officers in the place of each nipple. Her navel had stretched into a large mouth that was grinning deviously and leaking saliva from its sepia-toned bottom lip. Her head was slumped to the side, her eyes rolled up under her eyelids, mouth hanging open. Although she maintained her dance, her hands tracing her own curves down her flat stomach and between her legs; she was clearly unconscious.

Diverted by the hands and arms and the moist slurp-snap as the nurse raised her hand from between her legs, the officers didn't see what it was that she pulled from her vagina until it was too late.

The nurse fired off three shots from the small handgun before they had time to react.

"In-a-gadda-da-vida, baby," quipped the mouth in her stomach in a gravely, Wolfman Jack-like tone. "Donchu know that I lu-u-uv you?"

The first shot caught Tate in the throat and passed clean through. He collapsed immediately, clutching his neck and gurgling out a brief response as he hit the ground and writhed. The blanket he was holding fell over him.

The remaining officers drew their weapons and fired.

Aside from the bang of their revolvers, the night was quiet enough that the smack-smacking of their bullets punching through the nurse's silky flesh could be heard clearly. She didn't bother to wait for the last gunshot before she straightened, tipped over like fleshy Swiss cheese and hit the ground ugly.

When it was all over, Simmons and Carter ran over to the thrashing lump partially hidden under Tate's blanket. Simmons paused, knelt down, and pinched back the edge of the blanket. He could only look at his partner's face for a split-second before it overwhelmed him. Tate desperately tried to breathe as he gagged and choked on his own blood, grabbing at the mangled flesh where his esophagus used to be.

Reilly ran to his car and radioed for an ambulance.

"Officer down!!!!" he yelled into the receiver. "Get an ambulance here. Fast!"

McMahon and Shields approached the nurse's body with caution, stepping tentatively, arms held straight, but pointed down in text book, TV-cop style. She lay with her back, right shoulder and breast to them, twisted in a wildly beautiful pose.

She flinched once... twice...

McMahon pulled the trigger and fired into the ground, then lifted his gun and fired once more at the woman's head.

Instead of blood, the wound drained and spurted colors: reds, oranges, yellows, greens, blues, indigos, and violets. There was blood–real blood–pooling around her abdomen and chest, but from her head there were only colors, thick, frothy, and alive.

McMahon and Shields couldn't believe what they were seeing. Even as they watched the colorful liquid ooze five feet to the manicured lawn and soak into the dirt, their subconscious minds told them that it was impossible, that they must be seeing things, that maybe they were slipping. Each had his reasons for questioning his own sanity, and neither of them knew if the other had seen the colorful liquid. And they just might have seen two eyes and a smile float by in the ooze.

McMahon was going to play it cool until Shields said something. That was the safest way. Shields, however, was planning to do the same thing.

———

Leaping full-throttle out of the quiet, laughter came at them in varied pitches and volumes, suggesting very large and very small things lurking inside the building, things that didn't sound at all like people laughing, but almost. Whatever they were, they were busting a gut. The sound was flowing from every window and doorway along the front of the building, as if heads with open mouths were leaning out. It contradicted what the officers saw through the lit windows, which was nothing: a lamp, maybe a dresser, a bed, a few paintings of scenery. They could see a few feet into the unlit windows as well. Clearly, there was no one there.

The officers stiffened. The laughter had them ready to shoot first and shoot any-fucking-thing-that-moved. It wasn't as if "What to do when confronted with a gorgeous woman with eyes for nipples and a mouth in her gut" or "What to do in case of disembodied, inhuman laughter" was in the handbook.

Simmons, however, was beyond all that. Watching his partner gurgle and choke and drown in blood left him numb. The laughter tickled his inner savage and gave it an appetite for vengeance.

Carter was the first to snap out of "What the fuck!?" and snap right into panic when he realized that they were standing out in the open, completely vulnerable to… whatever was inside.

"Everybody take cover!" he yelled. The officers scattered. By the time anyone noticed Simmons, he was halfway inside the main doors.

Crouching behind their cars, they watched the door slam shut.

—

Old cartoon characters reciting trademark phrases was the last thing Simmons expected to hear when he entered the main lobby– laughing woodpeckers, smartass wabbits, a stressed-out Chihuahua in the middle of a meltdown.... It was coming from the doorlined corridor at the back of the lobby. There were three rooms on either side, blue light flickering from the doorways like high beams. All the televisions seemed to be on.

What was going on?

The long corridor intersected with another a few feet from the fifth and sixth rooms. There was an office on the other side, directly ahead. There were letters on the frosted window of the door; some sort of official title, he guessed. He was too far away to read it.

Simmons paid little attention to the lobby he was standing in. He could not have cared less about the antique leather furniture, the Italian chandelier that hung from the ceiling, the brown and white murals of "roarin' '20s" city life that decorated the walls, the wide, winding staircase that snaked upward to darker places.

The voices stopped as soon as his foot crossed the threshold from the lobby to the hallway. Static and pitch-bending radio frequency noise filled the void. And there was one more thing: the smell of fresh paint. It was a toxic stench, so strong that it stung his eyes. Strange, he thought, but currently it registered about a 4 on his "give-afuck" meter. Finding out who was behind what happened to his partner blotted out everything else.

Simmons came to the first two rooms and found nothing but an unmade bed and a television screen filled with static in each.

There were still four more rooms, and the office. He could read the letters on the office door now: Reigert Everhardt, MD. Settling into his surroundings, Simmons thought he saw things on the walls all around him, and the ceiling, too–cartoon characters smiling down on him. Their smiles shook the weight of whatever they were trying to mask. It looked like anger, or maybe disgust.

The characters were born of completely different styles and levels of talent. He recognized a number of them from his youth; back when credits with names like Chuck Jones, Tex Avery, and Hanna-Barbera were burned into his mind. Others reminded him of Ralph Bakshi, John Kricfalusi, and Frank Frazetta–a few favorites from his teenage years.

They have kids here too, he thought. Then he noticed the nudity, both male and female. What kind of fuckin' place is this?

A jumble of sounds indicated movement down the hall. It was coming from the office.

Snapping into position, his gun pointed, Simmons called out, "Somebody inn'ere?"

He turned his ear to the door and listened. The silence spooked him. It wasn't a dead silence, it was a weird marriage of static, emptiness, and feverish pounding.

"Don't make me have to come in there after you… whoever you are," Simmons warned the eyes peeking out from behind the office door.

18

They disappeared behind the office door in reaction. From his immediate left came a voice…

"Eh… I don't think he's coming out, bub."

Simmons whipped left and ended up face to face with the things on the wall. Only now, he saw frowns; pink lips peeking out from black faces. It gave him a jolt. He backed away and spun to check the wall behind him. Same thing.

"What's goin' on in there, Simmons? Talk to me, man!" MacMahon said into the front door.

Simmons suddenly felt ambushed, closed in. Somehow his eyes found their way back to the office door. The eyes were back. They were watching him hard.

He started to back away when paint from the walls rained down on and around him as if an invisible levee had finally been broached.

———

McMahon and Shields fell into the lobby and right on top of each other. Carter and Reilly followed them and planted themselves into position, their weapons aimed at the "thing" that coughed and flailed at the air in the middle of the door-lined corridor. From its feet up to its waist, it looked like a man wearing police blue.

Simmons? They wondered in unison.

From the waist up, the man was animated–a weird, elongated caricature of Officer Simmons. Whatever it was that had painted him to look like some bastard lovechild of Stephen Gammell and Peter Chung was creeping down his body and coloring the rest of him.

Simmons reacted to the commotion at the front door by blindly firing. His eyes were stung closed by the paint so he couldn't see who it was. And he couldn't see the makeover that the paint was giving him. The toxic smell burned the inner lining of his nostrils. The taste caused him to gag. His gun was big and fat, like a child's toy. Three bullets literally screamed out and bore down at the men with determination. From the side view, an anime blur indicated just how fast they were moving.

"Let's git dat mutherfucker," the bullet in the middle said.

"Get down!" Carter yelled, and the officers scattered.

The three bullets chased Carter to the floor and swarmed around him like angry bees. They were frowning and baring teeth.

McMahon, who was the closest to Carter, crawled away on his side. Reilly and Shields watched dumbfounded as the first bullet tore into Carter's left hand, which he held in front of him to defend. The others found his arm, shoulder…

Carter leapt to his feet and batted at himself with his good hand as he stumbled and bounced from wall to wall. He ran in circles, screaming bloody murder.

Shields took a chance and fired at the animated bullets. He hit Carter instead, three, four, five times.

"Shields!" McMahon scolded.

The animated bullets had just eaten Carter's head and were on their way down his torso and right arm. His body slumped to the floor, knees first. He leaned forward and began to fall.

There was nothing left to hit the ground, only tiny ribbons of flesh and fabric floating where Carter knelt. The three bullets disintegrated when they were done ravaging Carter's remains.

—

"Oh my God! What happened to me!?!" Simmons screamed. He was staring at his strangely drawn hands. He lifted them to his face and felt both sides of it. His fingers translated the distortion perfectly. To his own ears, his voice sounded fine. However, all McMahon, Shields, and Reilly heard was static and pitch-bending radio frequency noise coming from his mouth whenever he spoke.

They aimed their weapons at him.

"Is that... Simmons?"

"Can't be."

Realizing that he had fired on his colleagues, Simmons said, "Oh shit! I'm so sorry! I thought... I didn't know."

McMahon led the backwards retreat toward the door. They stepped blind, holding their aim on the Simmons-thing who talked like a bad transistor radio lost between clear signals.

"No guys, wait," he hurried toward them as he spoke. "It's me. It's Simmons."

"Don't come any closer!" McMahon demanded.

"It's me, Mac." Simmons pleaded. "I swear it is. I don't know what's going on but the paint... it fell on me and..."

"I said don't come any closer or I'll..."

"Jesus Christ, Mac!" Shields added. "It looks like Simmons!"

Somewhere in the lobby, a woman screamed. Her voice had an otherworldly echo.

The roarin' '20s' street scene came to life on the wall that bordered the stairs. A young blond nurse ran through the two-dimensional crowd of boys in knicker suits, men in pinstripes and bowler hats, ladies in tea dresses and beaded gowns. The white of her nurse's uniform stuck out in the dull brown and white mural that held her. From her upper right breast, a Harrington House logo called out in bright red letters.

A few of the men in the crowd tried to grab at her but missed. She continued to lurch through the pedestrians. Judging from the look on her face, she was running for her life. She seemed to be getting away until a lamppost with teeth reached down and snatched her up by the head. As she dangled, kicking and flailing, the street surrounding an open manhole below her turned pliable. The manhole stretched up from the ground, human teeth poking forward until they resembled those of a great white shark. The manhole bit down on her waist and tore her in half, then settled back into the street where it chewed and swallowed with a loud "GULP."

Simmons was jogging toward them now, looking over his shoulder at the wall alongside the stairs.

McMahon and the others found themselves flabbergasted once again.

Simmons was almost on them when he tripped and fell into McMahon, who put his arms up at the last minute. He braced himself for the approaching weight, but there was only liquid.

Simmons had literally splashed all over McMahon and soaked him to the bone.

"What the hell?!?" McMahon spit through the harsh-tasting sludge. He squeezed his eyes shut at the burning sensation and wiped himself feverishly. "Fuck! What is this shit?"

He reached out to Shields and Reilly. They quietly backed out of range.

"Shields... Reilly... I can't see. What is this stuff? Where's Simmons, er..."

The paint slithered over McMahon's torso and under his clothing.

"C'mon, guys. Gimme a hand!"

The paint around his chest began to stretch outward away from his body and into the shape of a cartoon character from the waist up–a rabbit that was familiar to all of them.

"Saaay, you need a hand, doc? How's this?" it said, cocking its arm back and slapping McMahon off balance with its oversized hand. He felt his jaw shatter and tasted his own blood swishing around the inside of his mouth along with a few of his teeth.

The rabbit just as quickly sank back into the living paint.

"Ahh," MacMahon shrieked, rubbing the paint away from his eyes. He opened them to a blur.

An infant wearing a fedora tipped to the side and clenching a stogie between his teeth emerged on his shoulder. "Or this!" it said, as it jabbed two tiny hands deep into McMahon's eye sockets and retreated into the paint.

McMahon screamed in response to the pain and

pressurized pop as the soft tissue splashed from his crushed eyeballs. Blood stole the voice from his throat.

The characters continued to come and go, emerging from random spots on his upper body. "Or this," each said in a voice as unique as the styles in which they were conceived. A devilish cat pulled out McMahon's tongue and sliced it off with a single, sharp claw; a shovel-jawed clown with Xs for eyes sprayed acid from a flower on his lapel and melted McMahon's face; a yellow, spikyhaired kid with an overbite slurped the liquefied flesh with a straw and spit the face fully intact (horrified expression and all) onto the wall.

Reilly planted his back against the wall and froze. Shields took off out the front door and kept going. As he watched McMahon do a spiral dance toward the hallway, Reilly spotted a set of eyes looking back at him from the cracked office door at the other end.

***

Hypnotized by the quick edits and the obtrusive colors that screamed at him from the television, the burnout formerly known as Dr. Reigert Everhardt sat in his shabby, one bedroom apartment watching the last fucking thing he ever wanted to watch: cartoons.

The last three years had been rough, ducking in and out of boarding houses and cheap motels. That night at Harrington House was still fresh in his mind, especially when he closed his eyes. He had seen the entire thing. He hid behind the door of his office and watched as the Coloureds (what the cartoons preferred to be called) murdered five nurses, eleven patients, and five cops.

Three years and he still couldn't shake the images and the voice that reminded him that it was all his fault. He knew that. Boy, did he know it.

It's all your fault… The words hurt like a sonofabitch.

Could've just as easily have been the Coloureds fucking with him, though. You wouldn't believe the kind of shit they pulled. People have the wrong idea about them based on what they see on television and in movies. That perpetually pleasant shit was just an act.

The Coloureds weren't bound by the same limits as humans. Unless specifically integrated into the personalities of the characters by the "artist," the Coloureds couldn't experience feelings like guilt or remorse. There was no right or wrong. Some had good natures and were willing to play by the rules; however, most of Coloureds were downright scary in person. They could bleed, lose an arm, a leg, even a head, and it didn't mean a thing. The only way that they could be killed was if they were erased.

Now, there were a number of ways to do such a thing, depending on the medium. Fire, turpentine, bleach, or good old-fashioned rubber worked against the Sketches, who were the slum-dwellers of the cartoon world.

The Coloureds will tell you that the art came before the artists. They pointed to the cave paintings to demonstrate that they communicated with early humans. Their numbers were few back then. Through their visual allure, they manipulated inspired especially perceptive humans (eventually known as artists) to fashion images, propagating their species and forming a bond with humans that endures to this day.

It wasn't until 1906, when J. Stuart Blackton made the first animated film, that the Coloureds started to become a force. A minority opinion held that the invention of the phenakistoscope in 1831 predated Mr. Blackton's invention. Before that, they were relegated to communicating through static images, with the exception of nighttime dreams and the waking reveries of the crazy, the religious, and the stoned. Because of their volatile nature, Coloureds rarely interacted with humans in person. Film and TV were the safest ways. "Only for the purposes of education or entertainment" was what the Interaction Treaty stated, which had been carefully drawn up and deliberated by leaders of both sides long ago. Except at the highest level, direct communication between species was not allowed. The underbelly of Coloured society (Sketches or Rough-Sketches) preferred it this way. They liked to fuck with humans in traditional ways, such as through hallucinogenic drugs. It was the Coloureds behind Swiss chemist, Albert Hofmann's accidental "trip" in 1943.

LSD was known to them as the "master key"; however, mescaline, psilocin and psilocybin, PCP, and ecstasy were popular as well, as were a variety of herbs and preparations from all corners of the globe. Such interactions almost always ended badly, so contact with humans through these means was officially illegal.

—

Everhardt first stumbled upon the world of the Coloureds in 1953 while working on project MK-

ULTRA (conceived by the Clandestine Services Department of the United States government to develop mindcontrol drugs) for the CIA at Edgewood Arsenal in Maryland. His concoction, TX-260, which was derived from henbane, was hailed as "the real super-hallucinogen" after tests with BZ (quinuclidinyl benzilate) by the Army Chemical Corps tests failed to produce "actionable results."

TX-260 was so potent that it left the user permanently intoxicated and susceptible to all kinds of suggestions and hallucinogenic distortions. "They seem aware of my existence," stated one of the test subjects while under the affects of the drug; other subjects made similar comments.

By the time Everhardt had completed lab and field testing of TX-260, project MK-ULTRA was losing steam.

The CIA pulled the plug on the program after a young woman confessed to reporters about her part in something called Project Midnight Climax. She provided the media with lurid details of sex, drugs, and espionage. Her claim was that she was paid by government agents to seduce men, bring them back to a motel that had been financed and outfitted by the CIA, and slip them LSD while military officials watched through a two-way mirror.

Everhardt never knew what happened to the test subjects as the project ground to a halt. He had a good idea what became of them, and he decided to leave it at that. He didn't want outright murder on his hands or his conscience. Sure, he figured, TX-260 fried their brains, but at least they were alive.

The CIA forbade Everhardt from taking anything when he left: not his research notes; not the remaining TX-260; not even the supplies and personal effects that he brought with him to the lab. Fearing that they might one day talk, the government quietly discredited all the scientists and medical personnel who worked on the project. A few of them just disappeared.

—

Warner Brothers found Everhardt in the early '70s. By then, TX-260 had made its way to Hollywood via self-destructive rock stars and counterculture celebrities like Timothy Leary and Dennis Hopper.

Warner Brothers was a hotbed of animation in the '60s and '70s. Coloureds who liked to interact with humans would often look to the Hollywood production companies for opportunities, as mixing for the purposes of entertainment was allowed by the Treaty. Disney was the people's choice, but they focused mainly on programming meant for young children, which required the Coloureds to tone down their language and antics. Mickey and the gang never heard the end of it. The Coloureds who found fame in the human world by obeying the humans, performing "clean" for the kids, and fostering images for themselves that were just as squeaky clean were decried as sellouts by their peers.

It was seen as a little more respectable to work for Warner Brothers. Warners had their rules and censors, but at least they had a knack for infusing adult humor into their animated shorts. It was a formula for success.

The Warners got rich–richer–and the Coloureds got their first taste of semilegitimate fame.

The Coloureds took to their status and power in the human world in the worst ways. They were always difficult to work with, but now, they were impossible. They saw the praise and accommodation lavished upon movie stars and felt that they deserved the same. Soon, rumors of after-hours parties, where Coloureds and humans could be seen brazenly drinking, fighting, and fucking together, hit the gossip columns.

The Coloureds got tired of languishing behind the scenes. Some began to resent the fact that the credit for the success of their films was always going to the human artists. All over town, tensions simmered. Some of the more aggressive Coloureds began to act out. Warner Brothers saw TX-260 as a possible way of controlling them, or at least reining them in. The troublemakers were well aware of the Treaty. If the Coloureds were willing to break them, they were going to have to pay.

The studio hired Everhardt to oversee their new clandestine operation; Project Toon-Out they called it. (Author's note: Clandestine operations were big in the '60s and '70s.)

During its five-year run, Everhardt watched the program spiral out of control. Coloureds were allowed to pass freely through the human world. The studios paid the news media big money to float "drug epidemic" pieces whenever someone reported seeing a "cartoon" walking down the street, or shoplifting, or raping their wife, etc.... If that angle didn't fit, they could always resort to suggesting "paranormal phenomena." The last resort was always an attempt to discredit the interlocutor using propaganda and misinformation in the form of "new developments" or "shocking revelations."

A new trend was emerging. Without a human host, a Coloured could only exist in the human world for up to 72 hours at a time. As a result, Coloureds were making under-the-table deals with ambitious but limited B- and C-list celebrities to share bodies in a state called "coexistence." Coexistence allowed the Coloureds to exist indefinitely, and for humans, it had a way of reinventing a person. Or at least it worked wonders for the complexion. And everyone loves an "animated" personality.

You'd know one if you saw one. They looked bizarre and sometimes horrific, like "after" photographs that were never going to end up hung proudly on some plastic surgeon's wall. Claims of botched plastic surgery were commonly made to cover up the physical marriage of a Coloured and a human.

There was one other way around the 72-hour limit. Some Coloureds took to robbing graveyards or finding worthy human candidates and waiting around for them to die, or in some cases, helping the process along. Afterward, they'd use the deceased human's body as a shell. But this way was even easier to detect as the "artificial" look was undeniable. Everhardt's list of suspects included:

1. Michael, Jermaine, Janet and Latoya   Jackson (especially Michael and Latoya)
2. Joan Rivers

3. The Barbie twins
4. Pricilla Presley
5. Melanie Griffith
6. Demi Moore
7. Dolly Parton
8. Lil' Kim

Legitimate coexistence was like living on a perpetual high, which was why so many celebrities turned to drugs and alcohol to try to hit the brakes on what was termed "fast living." Many of those in coexistence burned out or died young.

Everhardt had seen many of them end up as suicides. The program was out of control, and he wanted out. He knew better than to go public with what he knew, so he left the studio one afternoon and simply disappeared, like a ghost, into the population.

—

Everhardt managed to stay under their radar until that night, three years ago at Harrington House. They had done a good job of making him look bad, thanks to that TV movie. The movie (a Lifetime Channel hack-job starring Bruce Boxleitner as Everhardt) painted him as an out-of-control deviant and drunk.

Everhardt was keen on continuing his experiments with TX-260. He figured that the elderly patients would be gullible and easy to control, so they formed the perfect patient population. He'd deal with the moral ramifications later. Hollywood and the government taught him how to do that.

Everhardt's research yielded some unexpected results. TX-260 was evolving. It no longer needed a host mind to act as a bridge between worlds. It was as if the drug, in its liquid form, was a living doorway, able to stretch and grow and move like a sentient being.

Of course, the Coloureds were to blame. Apparently they had learned to control the liquid. The elderly folks who took the drug saw the Coloureds come to them as angels and demons, as ghosts and imaginary friends. The Coloureds seemed to enjoy the creativity involved in fucking with them.

Everhardt had to put a stop to the experiments. He locked the remaining TX-260 in a freezer and destroyed his notes. But some of the folks had caught on to what Everhardt was doing and what was bringing on the strange and powerful sensations. It was the clear stuff. The clear stuff brought the visions and made everything alive again. The clear stuff brought friends and comrades. No one was alone when the clear stuff was around. They had become addicted to the companionship. And Everhardt knew. He knew that the clear stuff made everyone happy, and that's why he took it away. A plot to raid the lab to steal the frozen vials made its way around Harrington. Things went back to normal—that is, until that night when the old folks rose up, and Everhardt went back into hiding.

—

The burnout formerly known as Dr. Reigert Everhardt had taken to watching the new girl across the hall in 203 through the peephole. Lately, it was the high point of his days, gripping him like a mini-addiction, all jubilant highs and terrible lows. It all depended on whether or not she was there when the sound of light footfalls or jingling keys brought him running to the door to look out. Her name was Christie Douglass, and she was married to a nervous-looking fellow named Burt or Burke. So far, that was all he knew.

When he was feeling especially lonely, he liked to think of Christie twisted into compromising positions. But that was only good for five minutes, tops. That was as long as he could last these days, at least with the furious pumping of his hand and a generous glob of petroleum jelly. He'd probably explode at the mere sight of a real, live woman standing naked before him.

But even the thought of that would have to wait until the cartoons were over.

Fucking Coloureds…

—

Hollywood's latest assassin was a no-talent rapper/ R&B crooner called Lil' Zeus. A few days earlier, Everhardt had rushed to the peephole after hearing footsteps, only to see Lil' Zeus making his way down the hallway, leaning his ear carefully against door after door, listening in. Everhardt recognized him from TV.

Lil' Zeus was one of those guys who belted out what amounted to sexualized nursery rhymes while trying too hard to frown his way into masculine poses. He liked to dance around shirtless trying to pass off his skinand-bone physique as lean muscle. He kept himself greased up and glistening, glossy lips pursed in pout,

Sharpe-rendered beard and sideburns laser-cut to fine edges.

When Lil' Zeus was just outside his door, Everhardt held his breath and shrank away. He shut off the lights and sat there silently watching the sliver of light beneath the front door, hoping to God that Zeus hadn't seen him. A pair of feet appeared, darkening the space. Everhardt could hear breathing through the silence–deep, heavy breaths punctuated by a stuttered exhale, suggesting arousal or maybe drug withdrawal.

It was only a matter of time until Zeus found him. Everhardt had no choice but to ask for help. The Coloureds were the closest thing to friends that he ever had. Friends or not, a favor from a Coloured came at a hefty price. He used to think that watching cartoons 24/7 was worth it. Currently, he was on hour 29. Until the job was done, and Zeus was out of the picture, Everhardt wasn't going anywhere–not for 43 more hours at least.

—

Everhardt leaned forward and arched his back to work out a cramp when large, beefy hands like damp, ice-cold catchers' mitts clamped around his biceps and pulled him upright in his seat. The goon-thing that stood behind his chair loomed down over him with its smooth face, long, droopy nose, and dot eyes. He called it a goon-thing because it reminded him of those things from the old Popeye cartoons that creeped him out when he was a kid.

The goon-thing made a vibrating hum. Although the

words weren't clear, Everhardt could sense a tone of frustration. Pointing at the TV with its big, beefy right hand, the goon-thing palmed the top of Everhardt's head with its left and forced him to watch.

***

Running through Clifton Heights in broad daylight probably wasn't such a good idea for a falling star of Lil' Zeus's caliber.

Traffic was backed up for half a mile as cars waited to turn from Springfield Road (where Zeus was) onto busy Baltimore Pike. Eyes snapping out of road hypnosis glazed over the small businesses and slant-roofed houses on either side of the road and the few people on the sidewalks.

"Hey! Aren't you…" a redheaded Asian girl said as Zeus bolted past her like a bat outta hell. He was clutching his right arm in his left hand and holding both close to his body.

She didn't seem to notice the blood on his clothing or that he was missing a hand. Nobody noticed. Or maybe they did notice and simply blew it off as being part of a video or a movie he was shooting. You never knew with celebrities.

"Oh my God! It's Lil' Zeus!!!" a different female voice cried out.

Zeus glanced over his shoulder. A late-model SUV….

Thank God!

He expected to see the car he was running from: an old, black Buick hoopty with tinted windows and two obese white Coloured girls inside. The word on the street was that Zeus liked the white women with the big arses. "Two-toilet-seat big," he liked to say. He denied it in the interviews, fearing a backlash from his target demographic of young black women.

"Pictures don't lie," his detractors would say, referring to the tabloid snapshots of Zeus, in disguise, sneaking into cheap motels to get his freak on with pear-shaped white girls.

"Why not just admit it," his (white) lawyer suggested. "It's 2006, for cryin' out loud. I would think people have moved past that sort of thing. Well… except maybe down south."

"It ain't just the south."

"Okay… the south and… and the midwest, then."

"I don't know what planet you've been livin' on, homes, but I catch muthafuckas screwfacin' me just about everywhere."

"That's probably because you lie about it. People hate liars."

"Whatever, man…"

Even if the girls weren't so big, and sometimes ugly, the fact that they were white was enough to make a lot of the sistas start hatin'. He didn't care so much about what everyone else thought.

—

Big and ugly was an understatement when it came to the Coloured white girls in the old black hoopty. Arm and shoulder fat squeezed out from the driver's side window like warm bread when the car pulled up to him in the motel parking lot and the tinted glass hummed open. He had just returned from another fruitless search for Dr. Everhardt.

From inside the hoopty, a throbbing beat caused the car to literally expand and contract, its outer skin pulsating and lifting from its frame and settling back in place. The driver flashed little yellow teeth pointing out of receded gums and hair jutting from her nostrils like antennae. It was the most busted smile he'd ever seen. Her skin was a strange shade of Caucasoid: blotchy, with obvious brushstrokes, as if she was painted in haste. He felt her enthusiasm even before he saw her. It was a feeling that he had grown used to, like a celebrity sixth sense.

"Hey, sexy." She leaned out the window and blew him a kiss. Even her voice sounded fat.

Zeus caught a glimpse of the passenger when the driver leaned back. She looked even worse.

Apparently, the disguise (a baseball cap pulled down in front and a bulky jacket) wasn't working. Or the hundred-dollar bills that Zeus used to grease the motel manager and the maid weren't enough for them to keep their fucking mouths shut about his being in town. The rags probably offered them five times that to rat him out. All it took was one sighting, and word was out. Some things never changed.

Zeus was going to ignore them and keep on walking. He thought about his situation. He knew how volatile the Coloureds were. Pissing these chicks off might somehow get back to whoever was in charge and fuck up his deal.

Zeus looked to see if there was anyone else around,

took a deep breath, and walked over to the old black hoopty.

"Oh my God, he's coming over here," the driver whimpered.

The passenger shook with excitement. The car rocked.

Zeus squatted and leaned toward the window.

"'Sup, ladies," he said, forcing a smile despite the nervous energy that had him fidgeting like a crackhead. "It's ah... nice to know I have such... beautiful fans like you two"

The driver was panting. The passenger was just staring.

"I just love your music," said the first fatty, flagging herself with her hand. "Cc-can I... Can I touch you?"

Zeus stuck out his hand. She took hold of it and puckered, her big lips folding into a wet meat tulip. Her hand dwarfed his own. Her touch was cold and damp, like wet paint. The fumes caused him to squint. He held his breath to escape the strong odor, looked away, and awaited the warm–or maybe it would be cold–touch of her lips. She was cooing like a fresh-stuck virgin surfing orgasm shockwaves. Coming from the obese Coloured bitch, it turned his stomach.

An explosion of sensation caused Zeus to yank his arm away from her, or at least try to. The girl had his arm in her mouth, pinched between her teeth. She clamped down when he pulled, teeth grinding and slicing through flesh, muscle, and finally bone. She was growling like a dog as she tore it away.

Zeus stumbled backwards gasping and staring in disbelief at the stump. It was, by no means, a clean break. Flaps of fibrous muscle and sinew drooped from the wound like heavily textured tongues overlapping each other and spitting blackened red saliva.

"I bet he tastes as good as he looks," said the girl in the passenger seat.

"Ummm-hmmm…" replied the driver, her cheeks punching outward. Zeus's severed arm twitched and flexed while she chewed. She finally swallowed enough to speak coherently: "Even better, gurl."

Physically, the pain registered as extreme cold, radiating up from the stump to the rest of his body. Delirium was challenging shock. Zeus fought back the wave of weird euphoria that he knew would only lead to him passing out.

The drainage from the stump slowed when he squeezed it with his hand, so he grabbed it as hard as he could, turned, and ran. His first thoughts concerned how this was going to affect his career and how bad (nappy-headed and ashy) he probably looked. Nappy-headed and ashy was right up there with death to a guy like Zeus.

"Where'ya goin', sexy?" the biter yelled, her voice interrupted by a deep belch that jumped up from her stomach and surprised her. "I thought you said I was beautiful."

—

Zeus managed to duck into an alley to wrap the stump with a dirty old scarf he found floating in the gutter. It was a bitch to knot using his teeth and his one good hand. It stopped the bleeding but brought back the pain, which was so intense that he vomited. Suddenly, he saw the hoopty at the far end of the alley and took off running again.

It was chaos when he hit the street. For the first time in his life, Zeus wished that he was anonymous, that he was just plain old Kenny Scruggs.

The blonde woman (wearing an Eminem T-shirt) who called to Zeus from the SUV had started a chain reaction of mostly women who leaned from their windows and stepped out of their cars to see the big star. There were horns blaring, girls and grown women screeching and carrying on as if the mere mention of his name brought them to orgasm. Zeus ran for a block and turned down a side street, then another, until he lost the crowd that was following him.

Why didn't I listen to Odell?

Odell Mitchell was his manager. He was always going on and on about Zeus's safety and preaching to him that all of his fast living was ultimately going to catch up with him, but he wouldn't have believed this shit. Lil' Zeus smacked his stump against the wall behind him over and over, then cradled it against his body, stifling his screams and sucking breath through clenched teeth.

Zeus was crouching in front of a fence that bordered a neighborhood and the back of a low-rent strip mall. He contemplated climbing it. With one good hand, it would be difficult, but he was determined to try once he caught his breath.

Activity from the front painted a picture of busy shoppers getting in each other's way in the parking lot. Hovering somewhere in the back of the noise was a muffled beat. Clifton Heights, like many suburbs of Philly, had lots of cars that spewed out muffled hip-hop or some R&B variant masquerading as hip-hop (the kind of music Zeus produced). Fuzzy speakers and ear-splitting volume usually made all the songs sound alike, but when he heard the chimes, then the church-bell, he knew it was the opening of his latest album. Next came his voice, speaking softly, supposedly into the answering machine of a girl he had cheated on. The unoriginal closing line of the message set up the following track: "You never know what you've got until it's gone."

—

Zeus straddled the fence, one leg dangling on either side. On the mall side, his pants snagged a broken link. He panicked and tugged on his leg, which only tore the fabric and got more of it stuck. He laid down flat on his stomach to keep from falling to either side. With one good hand, it was hard to maintain his balance. Getting to the top of the fence was a struggle in itself. His stump was throbbing.

The sound of his own music echoed down the corridor between buildings and back to where Zeus laid atop the fence, arching his ass in the air to keep his scrotum from being crushed under his weight. The music suddenly poured into the open space when the black hoopty bled slowly from the mouth of the corridor and crept to a stop thirty feet from him, its outer shell pulsating.

The sight of the car made Zeus tug faster. He

struggled. His leg had been cut by the fence and was bleeding, but he could hardly notice.

The tinted window on the driver's side bucked and began to ooze downward.

—

"I think I saw him come this way," the blonde SUV-chick squeaked. The pack of rabid fans followed her down the corridor. A few of them were screaming as they ran. One was crying and shaking.

Dead center in the clearing just beyond the corridor, the black hoopty sat diagonally with both doors wide open. Zeus's voice continued to pour from the stereo.

The SUV-chick was the first to reach the hoopty, the first to see...

Two animated fat chicks fighting over a man–Zeus. They were huge, maybe seven feet tall, and dressed in ghettofied clothing that looked about three sizes too small.

The driver had the kind of hairstyle that would've looked better on a black girl. She wore a halter top and low-rider jeans that showed the top of her thong in the back. Her fat ass devoured all but the triangular piece at the top, and even that was hard to see. It was so big that it bubbled over the edge of her pants all the way around to her exposed belly and flapped like a dimpled meat-wing when she moved. Her cleavage heaved and jiggled.

The passenger was just plain fat. Her hair was pulled tight into a short, dookie ponytail that curled under at the tip. She was wearing a T-shirt that read "Can't

Touch This" in bold letters and a skirt that barely hid the bottom of her droopy ass, which looked like a bag of wet mud. Broken veins and pimples decorated her lumpy thighs. They looked like they could snap a man in two with one squeeze.

"He's MINE!" the driver growled. "I saw him first."

"You just want 'em all to yourself," replied the passenger. "Now gimme!"

They each had Zeus by an arm. The driver had the stump. They held him off the ground between them and tugged on his body like children fighting over a doll.

Zeus was starting to fade. His eyes were rolled up; his mouth hung open. His face barely registered their tugging and twisting. The SUV-chick in the front of the pack caught his unfocued eyes and felt instant terror.

"I'm swear ta God I'm gonna hurt you if you don't let go," the driver warned.

"Well, I guess we goin' be fightin', then, 'cause I ain't lettin' go."

As they continued to tug, Zeus mouthed something to the SUV-chick. He repeated it over and over.

The rest of the group had either scattered upon catching sight of the scene or just stood there in a daze, trying to figure everything out.

The SUV-chick was shaking her head "No." No to the violence; no to the sight of two giant cartoons; no to Zeus's message, which she couldn't understand; and no to the buckle and fold of his torso as his skeleton broke into pieces underneath his skin.

She cupped her hands over her mouth and cried for him.

"D-d-d-don't l-look at meeee..." Zeus rasped once

more before he broke like a wishbone and split open from his left clavicle down to his right thigh.

***

The burnout formerly known as Dr. Reigert Everhardt awoke to the sound of his own breathing. He yawned away his sleep induced narcosis and allowed the new day to accept him. As usual, the facts fell into place clumsily, and with little concern for a sequential timeline; the Coloureds, Lil' Zeus. And, as usual, it left him lingering on how much he preferred the sleep-stupor to blunt reality– until he remembered the time.

He looked at the clock on his nightstand. The LCD display flashed 9:47 am. It was over... The Coloureds' 72 hours were up.

Halle-fucking-luiah!

When working with the Coloureds in this capacity, Everhardt generally preferred to be there to send them on their way when the gig was up. That way he could make sure that the deal was honored and, through his own eyes, confirm their departure. Once the 72-hour limit was reached, the Coloureds had no choice, but it reassured him to see it for himself.

Watching them break down (into a clear, gelatinous goo) was an unsettling experience as it was extremely painful for them. Sometimes it came out of the blue. They'd be in the middle of a sentence then, BAM! The next thing he knew they were screaming and thrashing about in a way that made the pain palpable to him. It only lasted a few seconds before their shape lost its hold and sent them splashing to the floor and leaving

Everhardt to clean up the wet spot, or spots depending on the level of assistance he requested.

His eyes had taken a beating from 72-hours worth of cartoon-watching. It had been so long since he last required their assistance that Everhardt had forgotten just how hard that part of the deal was. Besides, his eyes weren't what they used to be. He tried to stay awake to see the goon-thing and the fat-white Coloured chicks off, but sleep was more persuasive. As a result, Everhardt harbored a touch of anxiety. Had they done it? Had they taken care of this Lil' Zeus character?

He checked the living room first. He was looking for the wet spot, or possibly even a body. He told them specifically that he didn't want to know what they did to Zeus or how they did it. But the Coloureds were notorious practical jokers.

There was nothing in the living room. He turned on the TV for some passive listening and moved on to the kitchen, and bathroom. He was about to declare both empty when he slipped and feel on his ass just outside the bathroom door. He didn't need to look down at his hands to realize what the sticky substance that oozed through his fingers was.

When he put it together with the living, breathing Coloureds (especially the goon-thing) that he had seen just hours ago, the sticky substance seemed to him like blood, their blood. Looking at it that way gave him the creeps.

Holding his goo-soaked arms away from his body, Everhardt pinched his wet clothes off and hopped in the shower.

The hot water took him to a comfortable place as

he stood under the showernozzle with his eyes closed. He remained there until the water ran lukewarm. He would've stayed even longer, fumbling with the faucet to savor every last bit of heat, but he suddenly thought of Lil' Zeus and his comfort level dropped considerably.

Everhardt did little things around the apartment to distract his thoughts while he listened for a report on Zeus's death. The news was good for running that kind of shit over more important events.

It suddenly dawned on him that he never checked under his bed. That was where he kept the metal briefcase that contained his remaining vials of TX-260. He had no reason to think that it wouldn't be there, but he felt compelled to check just the same. His stash was his lifeline. The years had earned him a dependency, not on the chemical itself, but the safety that the things that dwelt within it provided. Sure it came at a price, but at least he was alive. At least he was alive....

If it came down to it, he could find more–the ingredients to make it, that is. It wouldn't be easy. First of all, he'd have to leave his apartment for an extended period of time. That was out of the question. The years had earned Everhardt an addiction to solitudel, topped off with a fear of crowds and an aversion to people in general.

Everhardt walked into the bedroom, got down on his knees and lifted the edge of the bedspread off the floor.

The briefcase was gone. And there was something lying in its place; a severed head. It was Lil' Zeus. His eyes were frozen wide open and staring right at him.

Everhardt gasped himself winded and dropped the

spread, his heart pounding like elephant footsteps. He waited a few seconds and lifted it again. Still no briefcase.

For a moment, (Oh!) Everhardt tried to cajole (God!) some forgotten memory of moving it to a safer place (No!). But he knew he hadn't.

As grizzly a sight as it was, Zeus's head was secondary to losing his lifeline. In fact, it didn't even faze him… yet. At the moment, Zeus was a non-factor, until he heard the newscaster mention his name.

"THE HEADLESS BODY OF TROUBLED RAPPER, LITTLE ZEUS WAS FOUND EARLIER THIS MORNING IN AN ALLEY BEHIND THE BARCLAY SQUARE SHOPPING CENTER IN UPPER DARBY, PA. A SURVEILLANCE CAMERA MOUNTED ABOVE THE FIRST TRUST BANK CAPTURED FOOTAGE OF THE MAN, WHO ACCORDING TO WITNESSES AT THE SCENE MURDERED THE RAPPER AND DISMEMBERED HIS BODY IN BROAD DAYLIGHT."

Everhardt ran into the living room, his eyes gunning for the screen even before he entered. He got there just in time to see grainy, surveillance footage of himself running from the alley. The version in the footage was slightly different, almost photorealistic, but not quite.

Coloureds!

Everhardt had been set up. But by who? Hollywood, the Coloureds, themselves?

On the screen, the image of a young blond (the SUV-chick) dressed in an Eminem T-shirt.

"THE BODY OF 22 YEAR-OLD JACKIE DERBIN WAS ALSO FOUND AT THE SCENE. DERBIN

HAD BEEN SHOT EXECUTIONER STYLE AND STUFFED IN A DUMPSTER."

The image cut to an old photo of Everhardt dressed in the suit he used to wear for special (informal) occasions. He only owned two at the time. The other one was for business.

"PHILADELPHIA POLICE HAVE ISSUED AN ALL POINTS BULLETIN FOR THIS MAN... DR. REIGERT EVERHARDT."

That was all Everhardt needed to hear before the moment became about keeping himself from loosing control. His blood ran cold. He backed away from the television as the old photo cut to a live witness, a man who looked quite suspect to him, like a Coloured living inside a dead human.

"I saw em' with ma own eyes," the artificial-looking man said. "He came running outta the alley all covered in blood like he was gonna..."

There was a knock at the door, a stern, confident knock. It sounded as if the person on the other side had big knuckles that were calloused over.

"Dr. Everhardt. This is the police. Come out with your hands up, or we'll be forced to break down the door."

Everhardt felt the room close around him and begin to spin. He was nauseous from the impact of losing his lifeline. His vision was fuzzy around the edges. The Coloureds had done this to him. To him... After all that he had done to bridge the cultures. After all the time he'd put into it. After everything that had happened to him as a result. He could've been a household name. Instead he was a recluse. Not even a recluse, but a prisoner.

"We know you're in there, doctor. Come out, NOW!"

He pondered opening the door and trying to reason with the officers. What would you tell them, he thought, that the cartoons did it. Yeah... Okay... Good luck with that one. Maybe you should just go out there and let those knuckle draggers put you out of your misery. What have you got to lose at this point?

Everhardt was desperate for the initiative to do... something... anything but stand there perusing the same places over and over hoping that the briefcase might suddenly materialize.

"This is your last chance, doctor. I'm going to give you 'til the count of three, then we're coming in. One..."

Throughout all his mental babbling, Everhardt's mind kept stopping on the bedroom dresser, like it was trying to tell him something...

"Two!" The officer's voice was revving up for something big.

Everhardt could picture the officer locking into his combat visage. Based on the voice he pictured a large man.

"One! Okay. Do it!"

The syringe!!! There was another syringe. Everhardt had left it under a stack of folded pants in his dresser drawer after using it to summon the Coloureds 79 and ½ hours ago.

A bombastic thud shook the door, the frame around it screamed under duress. Everhardt high-tailed it toward the bedroom. Behind him the door flew open and backhanded the wall next to it. The wobbly, brass knob left an indentation.

Two officers entered and immediately began to chase him. The faster of the two men dove for Everhardt's legs, wrapping his arms around them at the ankles and squeezing them together.

Everhardt had made it to the dresser, slid the top drawer open and reached his hand inside before he lost his balance and began to fall. The second officer tackled him at the waist on the way down, winding him.

Everhardt lay motionless, gasping for air beneath the two burly husks. His mind was scrambled by the second blow, the one that momentarily hyper-extended his back.

"His hands... Get 'is hands!" the officer at Everhardt's ankles yelled to the one who lay directly on top of him, palming his face into the dirty carpet.

He grabbed Everhardt's wrists to cuff them together and hesitated.

There was a needle stuck in the meat of Everhardt's thumb. The syringe was broken in half and it was empty.

The officer turned Everhardt's palm up and showed it to his partner.

"Heroine, PCP?" he questioned.

"Just cuff him," the other officer said. "Well figure it out later."

—

Everhardt came out of the daze with little knowledge of how he wound up on the floor, handcuffed. The last thing he remembered was the police breaking down the door. There was a burning sensation in his right palm, a funny taste in his mouth, like paint. His hearing was muffled, and filtered through his discombobulated brainscape.

About five feet in front of him, painted hands reached up from a colorful puddle that surrounded one of the officers's feet and slowly pulled him down beneath its surface.

"No!" Everhardt belted realizing that he was looking at the remaining TX-260 from the syringe. "NO! NO! NO! NO! NO!"

The officer fought valiantly, but there were too many arms. Each one was a different size. Some looked as if they belonged to animals or… something.

The other officer had hold of the sinking one's right hand. Dropping his stance and leaning back, he pulled as hard as he could. He kept holding on after his partner was completely submerged. The remaining officer's hand had broken the surface as well.

"Gaskins! Gaskins!" the officer yelled down at the liquid. "Hold on, brother. I'm coming in."

The officer took a deep breath, cheeks puffing out, and plunged his face down into the puddle to try and locate his partner.

Everhardt opened his mouth to warn the officer not to do it, but something literally had hold of his tongue. When his hand brushed against the wall he was propped up against, he felt something sticking out of his palm. He knew right away what it was.

The officer snatched his head from beneath the surface of the puddle and fell backwards. His eyes were as big as golf balls. He looked over at Everhardt as if to relay the horrors that he had just seen when he began to choke. He grabbed his throat, climbed to his feet and stumbled from wall to wall like a pinball.

A painterly hue suddenly overtook him from the feet up until his entire body was tainted with artistic embellishment.

Everhardt cried as he watched, not for the officer's fate, but his own. Using the wall for leverage, his back pressed firmly against it, he slid up to his feet and plucked the needle from his palm using his index and middle fingers.

The officer was tearing at his uniform as if he was still normal underneath it.

Wrong.

He cried out in pain as his shirt began to part. It felt as if his was tearing at his own flesh. Apparently the shirt had fused with his skin.

Everhardt moved stealthily toward the door as the officer dealt with his dilemma.

The officer's bones began to crack and reshape inside of him. He coughed up what he thought was blood, except it was multicolored.

He looked over at the wall where Everhardt was sitting, then whipped around to find him standing just outside the bedroom, his hands still cuffed behind his back.

The officer reached out to him, "Help meeeeeee…," he whimpered as he began to morph through a rapid-fire, Tex Averystyle shape-shifting montage of characters. His heavily altered features remained intact throughout each guise as if to verify beyond a doubt that it was him (the officer) looking out from each colorful facade.

Everhardt watched the guises come and go as he backed away. He saw:

A little girl in a frilly dress singing "A Trisket a Trasket" as she held a lollipop with a sneering face on it.

A dimwitted hilly-billy in the form of a bipedal dog dressed in overalls and singing "Oh ma Darlin'"

A caricature of a Chinaman speaking jibberish in some a mock-Asian dialect.

A Carmen Miranda-esque woman with big, red lips.

An Al Jolson inspired bulldog in a coat and tails.

—

The officer's terror shined through in the eyes of each guise. The feeling resonated out to where Everhardt was standing.

Everhardt turned and ran out the front door of his apartment and into the hallway. The walls were stained with smoky soot, scrawled pencil markings and years of neglect. For some reason it stood out more now than it usually did.

The DING of the elevator gave him incentive. He hurried down the hall and peeked around the corner. All clear. He ran up to the elevator and ducked inside just as the heavy doors were closing.

Everhardt fell against the rear wall and watched the descending numbers light up as the elevator glided down.

***

There was a reason why everyone called the two blocks between 52nd and 54th Streets, Homeless Row. The streets were narrow, and lined on both sides by the backs of restaurants and designer clothing boutiques. Dumpsters outside of each one served as a stabilizing wall for the cardboard and discarded wood domiciles that decorated the undergrowth of refuse. Rickety fire escapes zig-zagged up the surface of the buildings and appeared to touch the sky. A sweatyfunk mist lay heavy in the air and stung the senses of outsiders. Enough light passed between the buildings and down into the street that impatient folks looking for a short cut felt safe enough passing through. When they did, they pinched their noses shut and walked straight down the middle of the street. The residents of Homeless Row didn't seem to mind. If they weren't caught up in some seemingly one-sided conversation with empty air, or sleep, or passed out drunk, or high, or both, they took it as an opportunity to solicit money–for something to eat, they were fond of saying.

As far as the frazzled young worker bee of a woman who entered at 42nd Street with a little girl in tow could see, there was only one of them up and about– an older man. Aside from his disheveled clothing, he appeared too clean, his features too indicative of some underlying brilliance. There was something dangling from his wrists. It looked like snipped chain links leading up to a steel bracelet. The man was pointing and cursing at the dark crevices all around him. If she wasn't so late for work, the frazzled woman might have decided against entering.

"Just a second, honey," the woman said to her daughter as she paused to search for the pepper spray that she kept in her purse.

She wrapped her hand around it, kept her arm in her purse and continued.

—

The little girl wasn't even trying to keep up with her mother, whose hand she held. As a result, her gait was too wide for her short legs, causing her to bounce, her little head flopping.

"Look at that guy," the little girl chuckled at the man with the bracelets who stumbled down the block toward them.

"Now that's not nice, honey," the mother replied.

The man suddenly stopped, clamped his hands over his ears and squeezed his eyes shut.

"I'M NOT LISTENING TO YOU ANYMORE!" he yelled. "YOU'RE ALL WASTING YOUR TIME!"

—

Until he opened his eyes, Everhardt hadn't noticed the frazzled woman and her daughter. At first he thought they were Coloureds and took on an aggressive stance in reaction. It caused the woman to stop, turn around and hurry back to the opening at 42nd Street with her daughter bobbling in her tightened grasp.

The block lit up with sickening color as soon as the frazzled woman and her daughter were out of sight. Now that Everhardt was himself a gateway, the Coloureds flocked to him from the other side. Until he figured out a solution (which he was determined to do) Everhardt dwelt among the homeless, with whom the Coloureds had a long-standing relationship. This way, he didn't stand out.

RETROGRADE

"Show of hands. How many guys in the audience have gone out of their way a block or two just to follow a chick with a killer ass?" the comedian asked as he paced the long stage, radiating confidence.

Laughter from the crowd. The 3000-seat venue was filled to capacity. Several hands went up—too many to count.

"See what I mean?" the comedian continued. "We're controlled by our dicks. Any dude out there who didn't raise their hand is lying."

More laughter.

The man was clothed in the standard funnyman get-up circa 1995, which was the cool thing to do these days. He still used a hand-held microphone, too. He wore pitch-black goggles over his eyes for no discernable reason and never addressed the strange accessory. Nor did he acknowledge it in any way.

"One more reason why living the clean life ain't easy," he said to the crowd. "The straight and narrow. Keeping up with the Joneses. That's why I envy animals. Their objectives in life are simple. Eat. Sleep. Fuck. Do you know how many conflicts throughout history would've been avoided if man could lick his own balls?"

"Do you know how many comedians have done that same bit better than you?" a man called out from the audience.

There was some quiet laughter. Some "Ooos."

The comedian nodded, flashed a wry smile. Gave a look. *Good one.*

59

He stopped mid-stage, pivoted toward the crowd, and said: "This guy here's a perfect example." He was pointing at the heckler, a rather forgettable looking fellow in his mid-30s. "Imagine where he'd be if he could lick his own balls. Assuming he has a pair."

The crowd "Oooo-ed."

"Good comeback," the heckler jabbed sarcastically.

"If he had any balls, then maybe he'd be up here performing to sell-out crowds every night instead doing… whatever it is you do."

"I'm an accountant."

"Oh. *Excuuuuze* me. Whaddayou you pull in a year? Fifty? Sixty grand tops?"

"I make a decent living," said the heckler.

A shift in the crowd. Some people were beginning to side with the heckler.

"A decent living," the comedian scoffed. "I got shoes worth more than you, dude. My *shit* is worth more than you."

Several people booed.

"At least I'm not a fucking drug addict!"

There was some applause. The comedian's expression shrunk. His shoulders slumped. He looked around the room in disbelief.

"Why don't you take off the goggles, as a matter-of-fact?" the heckler added. "Mr. 'Clean and Sober.'"

The crowd became rowdy. Some people were slinging insults, instigating.

The comedian pursed his lips in anger, balled his fists. He heard several people shout for him to "Take off the goggles!"

"Yeah! Let's see your eyes," came another voice.

After a few moments of this the comedian's posture inflated. He reached up, snatched the goggles off, and thrust his face toward the crowd.

People screamed.

***

It had been a better than average shift, which suited Officer Dutch Jensen (pronounced Yen-sen) just fine. The streets were on chill. The weather was just right. And the college girls bar-hopping through University City were looking especially good tonight.

He was on the ass-end of his shift, waxing nostalgic for the good old days when people managed to get through life without the help of MODS with Officer Daniel Kosugi, his partner of three weeks, when the call came over the radio.

"All units. Possible hostage situation in progress at The Tower Theater at 69th and Ludlow. All units.

Theirs was the second unit to arrive at the Tower Theater, a staple of the Philly music scene. A crowd had gathered in front of the place, rumor mongering and such.

They ran in. Guns drawn. Posture on "I'll shoot your ass if I have to!"

They came upon the first team in the lobby. They were posted, backs-to-the-wall, on either side of the double doors that led into the main room. An angry voice coming from inside. One guy looked like he had gone a few rounds in an open-handed-bitchslap contest and was still reeling from the sting of meaty palms. The other one looked fairly normal by comparison, if not a little scared off his ass.

Normal cop gestured for Jensen and Kosugi to "take caution." And then he pointed at the holo-screen on the wall behind the concessions counter. A woman squatting behind the counter. An employee, presumably.

Jensen took one look at the screen, turned rightly puzzled, and said, "You want us to watch a fucking movie?!"

Normal cop quietly informed them that what they saw on the holo-screen was, in fact, currently happening in the next room. Concession girl came in with the assist.

The comedian was seated at center-stage wearing the signs of multiple blasts from a standard issue police amplitude gun about his torso.

Amp guns were revered by firearms aficionados for their stopping power and lauded by peaceniks who took issue with the devastating toll they inflicted on the human body. It was easy to see why it was nicknamed the "Hole Punch."

The comedian was still alive despite the gaping, cauterized holes, like fleshy-framed windows into his soft, squishy interior. He had the heckler's battered corpse seated on his lap like a ventriloquist's dummy, holding him upright by the scruff of his neck. The dead man's head was slumped, a wide-eyed shock-mask frozen on his badly bruised face.

But most shocking off all were the beams of ethereal light coming from the comedian's eyes, which were but empty cavities in his face. It looked like someone had literally cut them out of his head.

Much of the crowd was in shock and unable to process what was happening. Some probably thought it was part of the show. Some were too intoxicated to care.

Onstage the comedian was riffing on the heckler's voice with his own nasally rendition and shaking and nodding the dead man's head to facilitate the appearance of life. He was saying things like:

"*I'M* an accountant!"

"*I'M* satisfied with mediocrity!"

"*I* don't have the balls to reach for real success so I like to bring down other people who do!"

Jensen turned to his partner, "Tha fuck is going on here?"

Kosugi had nothing.

"That's Dirk Blankenship," concession girl explained, pointing at the holo-screen.

"The comedian?" a confused Kosugi replied.

The girl nodded and said: "Some heckler kept giving him shit during his show, and he just, all of a sudden, went off on the guy." She paused to find the right words. "First, he starts doing this with his hands, you know, like making a choking motion. And then the guy starts choking for real."

"The heckler starts choking?" Jensen clarified.

"Right there in his seat."

Jensen made eyes at the other cops in the room. *Is this chick for real?*

Kosugi was the only one who seemed to share his sentiment.

Next, he looked the girl in the eyes, and said, "So, Blankenship came down into the audience and—"

"No. That's what I'm trying to tell you. Blankenship was way up on the stage. He was somehow doing it—choking the guy—without even touching him. Then he starts punching and kicking at the air, like he's beating on somebody, and the guy—the heckler—he's reacting to all this like Blankenship was right there in front of him. You could see where he was being punched and kicked. You could hear the blows hitting the guy. He's getting thrown around and stuff. He ends up in the aisle, all bleeding and messed up. People are screaming and trying to get as far away as possible, but Blankenship wouldn't let them."

Jensen just stared at the woman as if waiting to be let off the hook.

"It's true," said the injured cop. "We found him in the aisle. He was being stomped like she said. I could see foot impressions appearing all over his body. I instructed him to get down on the floor. He ignored me and continued assaulting the victim. I informed him that I was going to shoot if he didn't comply. He continued, so I fired off 4 rounds with my amp gun. He shoulda been dead. But he doesn't go down. He gives me this look, points at me, and yells. 'Get out!' I felt hands all over my body, but there's nobody there. Then, I'm being thrown back out into the lobby. We've been waiting here for backup since."

When he was finished, the injured cop's face settled into a look that said, "That's my story and I'm sticking to it."

An uproar from the main room. All eyes were on the holo-screen.

"SIT YOUR ASS BACK DOWN!" Blankenship

yelled, thrusting ire at some random male fan that had made an attempt for the doors.

The fan cried out. People screamed as the man was forcibly returned to his seat by invisible hands that cared little for his comfort. Afterward, Blankenship returned to his dummy.

"The nerve of some people," he quipped in the dead heckler's voice.

Jensen reached for his handcuffs, but then remembered that he didn't have them. Long story.

"Your smart-cuffs," he said to the injured cop, but the man was too caught up in the TV show. "YOUR CUFFS!" he repeated.

The injured cop reached for his belt and handed Jensen a silver, plum-sized orb with a button on top. More buttons on a small, metallic faceplate on his belt above where the orb was secured by some kind of magnet.

Jensen took the thing, thumbed the button. A pin-point of laser-light appeared on the face of the orb.

Watching the holo-screen to ascertain the shifting direction of Blankenship's attention, Jensen crouched in front of one of the doors, dug his fingers into the sliver of space between the bottom of the door and the floor, and inched it open enough to slip the hand with the orb in it inside.

He peeked through the sliver and aimed the laser-light at the comedian, who was busy free-styling with his new prop.

He pressed and held the button on top until it beeped twice, and then tossed the orb into the air.

A woman seated at the back of the audience heard

the sounds and turned to investigate. She shrieked at the silver blur that whizzed by her head.

Jensen suddenly found himself swathed in ethereal light. His eyes became slits, laboring to adapt to the brightness as he traced the converging beams back to their source—two glowing pits on Blankenship's face.

"I said, 'GET OUT!'" the comedian roared.

Jensen extricated himself from in front of the double doors just as they flew open. He was suddenly overcome by ethereal light. It was so oddly bright that he could feel the heat from way out in the lobby.

Jensen felt cold, leathery hands on his person, snaking along the contour of his clothing, fingers probing and molesting. He swatted at the sensations. Nothing there.

But they *were* there. One of them clamped over his nose and mouth so that he couldn't breath. Large arms embraced him and squeezed out all the air.

Up on the stage, the silver orb stopped at a hover in front of Blankenship. And then, without warning, the orb separated into four equal parts. The debris found purchase around the comedian's wrists and ankles respectively, yanked him into the air, and held him there spread-eagle.

Screams when the heckler's body slid off his lap and hit the floor.

Blankenship growled in protest, and thrashed his head from side to side. Ethereal beams whipped around the large room like dual searchlights under the guidance of a raging meth-head.

Jensen collapsed into his partner's arms, suddenly free of the probing, prodding, molesting hands.

A stampede of terrified audience members ran screaming from the main room. Several people were injured.

Blankenship must've called the cops every profanity in the book as he hovered, spread eagle, 10-feet in the air. Normal and Injured cop were assisting the victims of the stampede. Some of them were in serious need of medical attention.

Jensen and Kosugi approached the stage to take the comedian into custody.

Jensen instructed the injured cop to, "Bring him down."

Injured was cradling some fat, half-conscious man in his arms, trying to make small talk to keep the man awake until the ambulance arrived. "It's gonna be alright," he said to the man, and then he pressed a few buttons on his belt, and snatched his hand away from a sudden painful sensation.

"SonofaBITCH!" injured cop cried out.

There was an electric hiss from his belt. Sparks.

"Shit," he said to Jensen, looking down at the thing. "Must've gotten damaged when I hit the floor earlier."

Jensen's eyes grew big. He ran and leapt onto the stage.

"Help me get these offa him," he said to Kosugi, who hurried onto the stage to assist as Jensen reached for the comedian's ankle.

Both men were well aware of what could happen when smart-cuffs malfunctioned. Somewhere, out there, there existed a clip of a man being torn apart by them. There was a movement to ban the damn things altogether.

Jensen touched the ankle-cuff and was hit with an electric shock that he felt in his teeth. It knocked him back and into Kosugi's arms again.

Blankenship continued to thrash and curse as the left ankle-cuff snapped open and fell to the stage leaving the other three to make up the difference, pulling and tugging to keep the comedian balanced in the air. A buzz-snap whirling sound accompanied the event.

The comedian cried out in pain as he was pulled and tugged in different directions. One of the wrist-cuffs snapped open and fell. The remaining two worked to accommodate.

Buzz. Snap. Whirl.

Jensen righted himself and shook off the lingering kiss of electricity. In those seconds, the other wrist-cuff snapped open and fell off of the comedian.

The remaining ankle-cuff jerked and pulled upward, struggling to remain airborne against the comedian's dangling, flailing weight.

"Help me!" the comedian yelled as he dangled, upside-down in the air, flailing and thrashing.

He was gaining success in his effort to weigh the lone smart-cuff down. To offset this, the cuff commenced a sudden free fall, and then an equally sudden upward thrust.

The comedian groaned at the pain in his ankle. His flailing and thrashing caused the ascending cuff to twist upward, snapping the man's ankle as if it was made of old twigs. He shrieked like a girl. The cuff kept going, swinging the helpless comedian up and over, and slamming him into the hardwood stage.

Buzz. Snap. Whirl. Thump!

There was a muffled shattering of bone. Errant blood spatter.

Blankenship made an "Umph!" sound, and then protested no more. The light in his eyes dimmed and began to flicker.

Jensen threw his arm up and turned his head away. Some of the blood got on his clothing. He hurried Kosugi off the stage and followed behind him.

Blankenship's body became caught in some kind of centrifugal loop as the lone smart-cuff worked to right itself against his flailing, and thrashing, which had diminished considerably. It continued to swing the comedian up and over, and slam him against the hardwood with horrific results.

A Rorschach puddle of blood and miscellaneous viscera grew with each wet, crunchy slap. Moist debris flying everywhere.

A woman screamed. She was among a group of the people who had wandered in from outside to catch an eyeful.

By the time the ambulance arrived, Blankenship's body was unrecognizable. The ethereal light had been extinguished. He looked somewhere between a deflated blow-up doll left in heavy traffic and a beige-colored garbage bag foraged by strays and spilling refuse.

The buzz, snap, whirl, thump had lost some of its vigor, but the lone smart-cuff still had enough juice left to maintain the centrifugal loop. Only now the impact from the comedian's body hitting the stage was more like the wet smack of one foot hopping through a rain-soaked landscape.

Jensen was standing at the back of the room, seemingly unimpressed. He had his arms crossed over his chest, suspicious eyes focused on the stage as he labored to fit square pegs into circular holes in terms of his understanding of what had gone down earlier. Funny thing was that it actually made sense in the grand scheme of things.

The paramedics had taken away the injured and the dead. Kosugi and the other cops were out in the lobby with even more cops, taking statements. It sounded like a madhouse out there.

The paramedics hurried back into the room trailed by a floating gurney. They headed toward the stage with a sense of urgency that Jensen almost found funny considering the comedian's condition. One of them slipped in some blood and fell on his ass.

A swell of voices from the lobby. Jensen heard his partner yell, "Hey! Stop those things!"

Seconds later, three disc-shaped drones flew through the doors and spread out to cover the entire room. A light flashed on the front of each one as they crept toward the stage.

"Great. The media's here."

***

Later…

The light turned green. Jensen stepped on the gas.

He had hung around the station for an hour or so after his shift ended. He bonded a little with his new partner and recounted the Tower incident upwards of 50 times. The guys were throwing out theories left and right. Jensen had two of his own.

Theory 1: MODS

Human-machine interface was a fairly new industry, having (barely) passed the testing phase only two years ago, and having done so under protest of top scientists and medical professionals who stressed the need for further study. Augmented living was a luxury of celebrities and the super-rich. But it was still in its infancy and a far cry from the super-human enhancements that all the futurist writers had promised. So there was no way it could explain someone sustaining multiple blasts from an amp gun or hollow eye-sockets that gave off light. And from the looks of it, the comedian didn't have any MODS, anyway. Jensen would have to wait to hear back from the coroner to be sure.

Theory 2: More a collection of loosely connected details than a bonafide theory.

-The sudden rise in violent crime with a focus on the eyes
-Perps who (like Blankenship) seemed almost invincible
-The serial killer nicknamed Mr. Bright Eyes
-All the damn Satan worshippers
-The tabloid headlines about aliens with glowing eyes
-His reoccurring nightmare

There was a bigger picture here that Jensen wasn't seeing and that bugged the shit out of him. But it was late. He was tired. His head throbbed from thinking too much.

Jensen activated "Autodrive," reclined his seat, and vegged out to the local News on the picture-in-picture window in the windshield. He was particularly interested in how the media would spin the Tower Incident—Blankenship being an A-list celebrity and all. Even if he was on a downward spiral.

His favorite anchor smiled at him, put him at ease. She was hosting some special about a collection of meteorites from Mercury that had been stolen from the Academy of Natural Sciences last year. Jensen would have found the show interesting had he not seen it a million times.

Jensen had a visceral reaction to the mention of the Tower Theater. It came on the heels of a commercial break, a quick tease about Dirk Blankenship, the comedian with the troubled past playing to a packed house for the first time since leaving rehab with a clean bill of health.

He waited for some mention of the incident. Instead the News cut to street interviews with satisfied fans as they left the theater. One of those interviewees was a man Jensen recognized, a middle-aged, chocolate-skinned fellow with Master Po eyes.

Jensen sat forward, coughed up words, "It's him!" The nightmare flashed across his mind.

Jensen's Nightmare

Nineteen-ninety-something...

Two men stand over another, a chocolate-skinned man, slumped in a chair, wearing a vest of leaking plasma wounds. One blast had torn away a third of his throat leaving his head to dangle upside-down over the seat-back, connected by exposed vertebrae and not much else. Blood flowed from the stump, running downward, up the man's face and over nearly-almond eyes with piercing white irises.

The two men wear stock disguises, like something the department might put together in haste. One looks like an Appalachian thug, the other like a denizen of an '80s Ninja Movie, unmasked. Smoking guns in their hands.

Their voices give away their identities.

"Shit! Man! You sure you saw something?" the thug says in Jensen's voice. "Cause I don't see a weapon."

"I thought... I mean... I saw..." says a nervous Kosugi.

"You saw what?!"

Kosugi hesitates.

"What did you see?!"

"It looked... like he had hooves."

"Fucking hooves?" Jensen says. And then he crouches and lift's the dead man's foot into view. No hooves. "We just killed an unarmed man."

Jensen and Kosugi are sitting in an unmarked Ford Sedan sometime later. The pitter- thud of heavy rain smacks the roof of the vehicle.

"If they connect us to this, we're done," says Kosugi.

"They won't connect us," Jensen half-heartedly assures.

Screams from outside the car. Jensen switches on the laser-wipers.

They are parked somewhere in the city where residential and commercial collide.

A naked man runs out into the street screaming "HELP ME!" He has one hand on top of his head to keep it from falling off his shoulders, but it appears oddly shortened as much of his neck is missing. His face and his naked torso are painted with sloppy strokes of red. His chest and stomach are peppered with gaping holes. Bulbous organs playing peek-a-boo.

People in the distance turn toward the noise.

"Is that?" Kosugi starts to say, knowing full-well that the naked runner is none other than the chocolate-skinned dead man.

"Yeah."

"But how?"

"I don't know. But we've gotta do something."

Kosugi is especially confused. "He took his clothes off?" he said.

The chocolate-skinned dead man weaves between parked cars, leaps over bushes, and darts through manicured lawns trying to evade Jensen and Kosugi. He lets go of his head to maintain his balance and it falls and dangles upside-down and bounces against his back. He trips and stumbles over obstacles, unable to see them. People scream.

They finally capture the dead man and lead him to the car. Kosugi restrains his arms behind his back, while Jensen has a hand on the man's head, struggling to hold it steady as he jerks and resists.

"HELP ME!" the dead man yells to the looky-loos watching from afar. And then, in the same breath, he taunts the two cops in a lowered voice, "Sure are a lot of witnesses. Just takes one of them to finger you and it's bye-bye career." He's got a quiet-cool demeanor. He directs that icy demeanor at Kosugi, whose grasp on the situation appears much less firm. "That's 12-years down the drain."

"How'd you know how long I've—" says a startled Kosugi.

Jensen slaps a hand over the dead man's mouth, says, "Ignore him!"

Someone screams.

"What's happening?" says some startled old matriarch standing at the edge of a nearby lawn wearing a bathrobe. "What's wrong with that man?"

"Yeah... our friend..." Jensen says, thinking on the fly. "He... had a little too much to drink and fell down."

They walk the dead man to the back of the car and open the trunk. The man bucks and screams into Jensen's hand as they force him inside the trunk and slam it shut.

The drive was scored by fists pounding on the trunk from the inside and a medley of taunts leveled in the voices of Kosugi's loved ones.

"How many times we gonna do this dance before you boys realize who you're dealing with?"

"What's that supposed to mean?" Kosugi whined. "What the fuck is going on here, man?! What the fuck is happening—"

"I DON'T KNOW, GODDAMMIT!" Jensen roared over gut-busting laughter from the trunk. "I don't know what it means! And I don't know what's happening! But if we're gonna make it outta this, we're just going to have to accept it, and focus."

"You won't make it," the dead man quips in Kosugi's wife's voice. "Just like the last time. And the time before that. And the time before that. And—"

"SHUT UP!" Kosugi yells.

"Hey Dan," Kosugi's wife calls out from the trunk. "You know that trainer I've been working with?"

Kosugi snatches his gun from the holster.

"Don't listen to him," Jensen warns.

"The one that you're sooo jealous of," she continues. "I fucked him. We did it in our bed. It was sooo good. Much better than you ever were. I even let him stick his big cock in my ass."

"Sugi! Wait!" Jensen yells as his partner jumps from the car while it's still in motion. He slams on the brakes, gets out, and goes after him.

Kosugi runs around to the back of the car and yanks the trunk open. The dead man attempts to sit up and is met by repeated blasts from Kosugi's amp gun. Limbs flail. Blood leaps from the trunk. The car rocks from the punch of an amplitude beatdown.

Jensen runs up and grabs his partner from behind. "No! Sugi! You'll draw attention to us—"

Suddenly...

Bright light from behind. So bright it's blinding. Voices lunge at them.

"FREEZE!"

"DROP YOUR WEAPONS! NOW!"

Three squad cars parked 20 feet away. Bulky silhouettes peeking out from behind them.

A moaning sound from the trunk of the unmarked Ford. An arm reaches into view.

"Wait! We're cops!" Jensen yells and reaches in his pocket for his badge.

The police open fire.

***

Jensen headed straight for the kitchen cabinet when he arrived at home. That was where he kept his libations. He poured a glass of Absolut and gulped it down in one manly swig.

He was lost in his head, reeling from what the News had told him and from the stare-down with the chocolate-skinned Master Po eyes of his nightmare.

He started to pour another glass, and then decided he'd rather drink from the bottle. He snatched it off the counter, walked into the living room, and knocked it back.

Afterward he looked around the room as if the answers he sought would materialize from the walls. He noticed something on the coffee table that he was certain wasn't there when he left for work that morning. It looked like an unlabelled DVD case lying on top of a manila folder stuffed with papers.

Someone had been in his house.

Jensen dropped the bottle and snatched his gun from the holster. He performed a thorough sweep of the place. Then another. He ended-up standing in front of his house, reluctant to go back inside until he had some idea what was going on. But there was nothing other than the belief that this, the Tower Incident, and the chocolate-skinned man, were, in some way, related.

Jensen eventually went back inside. He picked up the DVD case and opened it. There were two discs inside labeled in black marker.

The first one read 'The 62nd Attempt.'

The second one read, 'Wide Awake!'

He would need to have the boys at the station run it through the digitizer to watch them since nobody owned DVD players anymore. He went to pick-up the folder and caught something else in his peripheral vision—a large, circular scorch-mark on the carpet in the corner of the room.

Jensen walked over and crouched next to the mark. Something had indeed scorched a perfect circle into the carpet. He poked the scorched area with his finger. It was still warm.

A glint of green caught his eye within the circumference of the circle. He nudged it with his finger, then picked it up. Some kind of jade charm in the shape of a teardrop attached to a red string.

VIDEO #1: The 62nd Attempt

A small, nondescript room. No windows. Old furniture--a couch and a club-chair facing each other. A coffee table between them. A timestamp at the bottom left corner of the frame reads: JUL. 3. 1994, 11:02AM

A chocolate-skinned drug dealer somewhere in his 30s is seated in the club chair as two men enter the room and sit next to each other on the couch. One looks like an Appalachian thug (Jensen). The other looks like a denizen of an '80s Ninja Movie, unmasked (Kosugi). Jensen is carrying a briefcase that he places on top of the coffee table.

The chocolate-skinned dealer looks wise, but menacing. He wears a cold expression that is hard to read. White irises.

Jensen: *We were starting to think maybe you didn't exist.*

Dealer: *I know you boys were looking to meet sooner, but, you see, I make it a point never to do business during the retrograde. I hope you two took precautions.*

The dealer's demeanor is quiet-cool, with a voice to match.

Jensen and Kosugi share a look. It's obvious that they don't know what he's talking about.

Jensen (lying): *Of course we did.*

The dealer smiles.

Dealer: *That's good to know. It's true what they say, that things aren't what they seem when Mercury does its backward dance. The media wants you to think it's all a myth, but don't you believe it. You can read all about it on—*

79

Kosugi (interrupts): *No offense. But can we just get on with the deal?*

The drug dealer stops talking. His white eyes roll over to Kosugi and settle into a glare.

Jensen: *Please excuse my partner. He's a bit impatient.*

Dealer: *Impatience can get you killed in this business. Or worse.*

Jensen makes a face at his partner, urging him to apologize.

Kosugi rolls his eyes.

Kosugi (half-heartedly): *Sorry about that.*

Dealer: *Your apology means shit to me, son.*

An awkward moment.

Dealer: *Let it be by thine action that I shall be judged and not by thine words.*

Kosugi: *What's that, from the Bible?*

Dealer: *I made it up. But it's a philosophy that I live by.*

Jensen leans forward, eager to get on with the deal.

Jensen: *The deal was for 5 vials of Wide Awake for 500 large.*

He slides the briefcase forward and opens it. Stacks of money inside.

Jensen: *Here's the money. Now let's see the stuff. Enough-a-this dancing around the subject bullshit.*

The dealer looks down at the money, and then back up at the two men.

Dealer: *You gentlemen ever hear the one about the guy who was gonna swim with a great white shark just to prove that they're misunderstood?*

Jensen shares a moment of gestural dialogue with his partner before turning back to the dealer.

Jensen: *Lemme guess. He got eaten.*

Dealer: *He was robbed and beaten to death outside of a bar two days before he was supposed to make the swim. You see, boys... the universe is a living, breathing entity. And just like your body has antibodies that help fight off sickness and disease, the universe has a way of rooting out potential disturbances to the natural order of things.*

Kosugi (annoyed): *So, the universe killed this asshole?*

Dealer: *Is that so hard to believe? We spend so much*

time and energy trying to combat things like crime, poverty, greed, indulgence, but, you see, it's those things that make the world go round. Take this guy I knew - a cop who thought it was his mission to save the world from the scourge of drugs. And where did it get him? Floating face down in the Schuylkill River.

A few seconds pass

Dealer: *Maybe you boys knew him.*

The remark unsettles the two men. They spring to their feet, guns drawn.

Jensen: *FREEZE! Police!*

Kosugi: *You're under arrest, asshole! You heard the one about the long-winded drug dealer who got pinched?*

The chocolate-skinned Master Po-eyed dealer appears completely unfazed by the two men standing over him with their guns aimed squarely at his forehead. He calmly leans back in his chair and crosses his legs.

Dealer: *I'm afraid I'm not familiar with that one. Please do enlighten me.*

Kosugi reacts in terror to something down by the dealer's legs. Jensen reacts to his partner's sudden start.

Static fills the screen.

***

"What happened?" Kosugi said.

"That's where the footage ends," Jensen replied.

They were in the station's AV room, standing in front of a floating rectangle of static being projected from a smooth, glass console with a flat, iridescent keyboard underneath. Jensen wore a messenger bag strapped across his torso.

"You called me in here to show me a 32-year-old bust gone wrong?"

Jensen moved closer to his partner, lowered his voice. "You don't recognize the guys from the footage?"

"Should I?"

"What if I told you that it didn't happen 32-years ago," Jensen proposed. "That it happened as recently as three weeks ago. In this district?"

Kosugi wrinkled his face, aimed it at Jensen. "What are you getting at?"

"Just answer the question."

"You alright?" said a concerned Kosugi. "I think the captain would understand if you wanted to take a few days off after last night."

This wasn't the first weird curveball that Jensen had thrown this morning. Kosugi had spent the better part of an hour convincing his partner that the Tower Incident *had* been covered on the News last night and that there was no street interview with a chocolate-skinned black man with white eyes. He had been watching the same channel and that's something he would have definitely remembered.

"I'm fine," Jensen replied. In fact, he was in serious need of sleep.

He stood there pressing Kosugi with his blood-shot eyes.

"We woulda known about any bust goin' down in the city," Kosugi acquiesced. "That's aside from the fact that the date was right there on the footage."

Jensen blew out some air, pondered. Then he reached into the bag strapped across his torso, pulled out a manila folder stuffed with papers, and handed it to Kosugi.

Kosugi took the file, "What's this?"

"It was with the DVD. Files on a drug called Wide Awake."

"Wide Awake?" Kosugi said as he opened the file and looked through it. "Never heard of it."

"You sure about that?"

Kosugi looked up, locked eyes with Jensen. "What's that supposed to mean?"

"Just think for a minute, dammit! Think! It'll come."

Kosugi frowned at Jensen's outburst, but ultimately decided to humor him. He pantomimed thinking deeply.

"I'm serious, man."

"Okay. Okay."

Kosugi straightened his face, searched his thoughts. Thirty seconds passed. A minute. And then...

A spark of memory. Kosugi's eyes lit up.

"You *do* remember. Don't you?"

"I don't know. I feel like—"

"—like Wide Awake had some significant meaning

to you. But you can't remember why."

"Yeah... Something like that."

"That's how it started for me, too," Jensen said. "But I've been reading through the file all night and watching the videos, and now I'm starting to understand."

"You said there was a second video?" Kosugi asked, wanting to know more.

Jensen typed something into the keypad. An image materialized from the floating rectangle of static.

VIDEO #2: Wide Awake

A narrator speaks over a montage of research footage and security camera clips from a government research facility.

Narrator: *It was synthesized from bacteria extracted from the Mercury meteorites. A miracle drug that was supposed to be the cure for blindness. But it never made it past the testing phase.*

- Four blind test-subjects seated in a room.
- The test-subjects react to being able to see for the first time.

Narrator: *The subjects could not only see again. They could see through objects; walls, skin.*

-A formerly-blind test-subject seated at a table on either side of a fake wall built for the test. They are each facing the wall. On the right, oversized cards with

simplistic shapes on them lay face-up on the table. On the left, similar cards in a stack, face-down. The left subject lifts a card from the stack and holds it up to the wall. The right subject points to the corresponding cards laying face-up on the table. The subject picks the correct card time after time.

-Split-screen. In one frame, a male subject is leering at a wall, masturbating. In the other frame we see a female subject changing clothes in her room.

Narrator: *Soon they were able to see beyond the normal visible spectrum. Radio waves. Soundwaves. Ultraviolet light. Infrared.*

- Subjects react to their enhanced visual realm with acid-trip whimsy. The waves are represented by colorful, squiggly lines crisscrossing in the air.

Narrator: *They developed an extreme sensitivity to light that resulted in one of the subject's eyes literally being burned out of his head when he tried to escape the test facility.*

- A test-subject runs up to a door at the end of a dark hallway. His eyes are literally glowing in the dark. He opens the door and screams as the sunlight instantly burns his eyes out of his head.

Narrator: *Another one extracted his own eyes after he didn't sleep for a week straight because he could see through his eyelids.*

- A doctor walks in on one of the test subjects standing in front of the bathroom mirror. A scalpel in his hand. Blood everywhere. The test subject turns to face the doctor. Empty cavities where his eyes should have been.

Test subject (terrified): *I can still see.*

Narrator: *They pulled the plug on the program after that. The remaining test subjects were weaned off the drug and released.*

-Anonymous research staff wheel the dead bodies of three of the test subjects into a refrigerated room. We see that each of them has been shot in the head.

Narrator: *All but one of them, who they continued to experiment on in secret. He claimed, after prolonged use, that he could see into a parallel dimension, a horrible place that reminded him of all the worst depictions of Hell he'd ever heard as a child. According to the subject, this place was populated with, things… similar to what we'd call demons.*

- The young male subject is throwing a tantrum in the cafeteria, yelling at the empty air all around him, and thrashing about as if trying to fight off multiple attackers.

Narrator: *These things, they were always looking for a way into our side to wreak havoc. This time they used the rift the drug had opened through his sight to slip through.*

- The young male subject is seated at a table. His eyes are too big for his face. He looks like he has seen too much.

Subject (detached, vacant): *They have hooves for feet. They dress like pallbearers with skin like shrink-wrapped leather, Xs for eyes, and sphincter mouths. And they want nothing more than to torment us.*

Narrator: *When the last test subject found out what had happened to the others, he struck a deal with these... things and they helped him to escape.*

- The male subject walks down a dark hallway, his eyes aglow with beams of ethereal light. Security guards have their guns drawn and pointed at him, but he continues forward, undeterred. As he reaches them, an invisible force disarms each guard and tosses them against the walls. We catch a glimpse, in a mirror, of the shrink-wrapped-leather-skinned, X-eyed, sphincter-mouthed things responsible for the 'invisible force.'

The screen goes black.

***

Jensen fingered some keys and the floating rectangle vanished.

"Was that you narrating the thing?" asked an incredulous Kosugi. He didn't know what to think. He wanted to laugh at just how ridiculous this all was, but he was unable to do so. Somehow he knew it was the truth. It was written all over his face.

"Apparently so," At this point Jensen seemed only slightly disturbed by the detour into left field that his life had suddenly taken, having reached some level of acceptance late last night. "The drug eventually reached the street level dealers. And that's when all hell broke loose. We were on the road to stopping it, when something happened..."

"We?" Kosugi said.

"Look at the photo at the back of the file."

Kosugi pinched the edge of the photo and slid it out from under the stack of papers. He held it up to his face and gasped a second later.

"That was us in the video?" he said in disbelief, and then he held the photo out for Jensen to see.

It was an old black & white photo of Jensen and Kosugi taken in some '90s-era police station. They were standing next to each other, playfully showing off their new disguises. Jensen looked like an Appalachian thug. Kosugi looked like a denizen of an '80s Ninja Movie, unmasked.

Jensen nodded. "That's what I'm trying to tell you."

Kosugi suddenly felt light-headed and needed to sit down.

"Remember the nightmare I keep having, that I told you about?" Jensen said. "I'm pretty sure it's what happened after the clip ended. I think we've been on this case for a *looong* time, partner. Longer than either of us care to remember. Somehow we keep getting stuck. Whatever that means."

Kosugi held his face in his hands. "This is *SO* wrong," he said in a muffled voice.

"I'm thinking the comedian and all the crazy shit on the News are signs that it's happening all over again," Jensen speculated.

"*SO* fucking wrong."

"The whole thing's a fucking mind scramble. Trust me. I know. I've been trying to wrap my head around it all night."

Jensen reached into his bag, pulled out a piece of paper with handwriting on it, handed it to Kosugi, said, "This was in the file, too."

Kosugi looked up. On the paper was an address scrawled in pen. A cryptic message written beneath it.

229 MELLICK STREET
STOP HIM!!!

A week later...

Jensen checked his amp gun, and then slid it into the holster underneath his blazer. Next he fumbled with the tiny camera disguised as a button sewn to his jacket to make sure it was secure.

"He's gonna try to get inside your head," he warned. "So, stay sharp."

"I will," replied Kosugi, who was doing the same thing.

They were parked in an alley on Mellick Drive, sitting in an unmarked Honda SUV. Jensen had flat-out refused the Ford Sedan that the grease monkeys at the station first rolled out of the garage. He cited his nightmare as the reason, but only told Kosugi that. He gave the grease monkeys some bullshit about Fords being unreliable, which, to the grease monkeys, was like saying he was down with pedophilia.

"Once we're in there, there's no turning back," Jensen said. "No matter what they might throw at us. You okay with that?"

"I'm good. But I won't be if you keep fucking harping on it."

"Fair enough."

Even now, with a week to scrutinize every word of the file, every photo, and to rewatch both videos ad nauseum, their grasp of the situation was shaky at best. Jensen was worried about his partner, who appeared somewhat disengaged, like maybe he was having doubts.

Jensen had been there, too.

"Got your back-up?" he said to Kosugi, breaking the silence.

Kosugi hiked up his pant leg to reveal a mini plasma-revolver holstered at his ankle.

"A PR 9, hunh?" Jensen commented.

"Why? What are you packing?"

Jensen lifted his knee, tapped his ankle, "Same."

A phone rang.

Jensen pulled the ringing phone from his pocket and checked the screen.

"Showtime!" he said and slid the phone back into his pocket. He grabbed a briefcase from the backseat and then motioned for the door. "Remember. If, at all possible, we want this guy alive."

Jensen knocked on the old steel door marked 229. Seconds later the door opened and a shifty-looking man stuck his head out.

Jensen smiled, "We're here to see—"

The shifty-looking man shushed him, and then he pointed at the sky, and said: "Eyes and ears everywhere."

Afterward he looked the two men over, and then pushed the door open with one arm and invited them inside with a nod.

"You guys ain't exactly easy to find." Jensen attempted to make light conversation as the shifty man led them up a flight of stairs and down a long, dank corridor that was barely lit. But the man kept ignoring him. "What? Is it just you two here?"

No response.

"As highly recommended as your man comes, I'da thought you guys would have this place sealed up tighter than a nun's asshole," he continued.

The shifty-looking man stopped walking, turned to face Jensen, said, "You talk too much."

Jensen put his hands up in surrender. "Just trying to keep it friendly."

Kosugi was ready to provide back-up, while trying not to look like a threat.

Shifty glared at Jensen without responding, then said as he turned around and started to walk, "Well. Keep it to yourself. Friend."

Jensen and Kosugi shared a look.

They came to a door at the end of the hallway and around another corner. Shifty turned to the men, said, "Only one of you goes in."

"No way! That wasn't part of the deal!" Kosugi protested.

Jensen put a hand on his partner's shoulder to

silence him, said, "I'll go."

"What?! No!" Kosugi whined. "We both go in!"

Jensen gestured to Shifty to *Hold on a minute.* Then he pulled his partner aside and spoke to him in a lowered voice.

"No turning back. Remember? I've still got my backup. I'll be fine. You just be ready to come in there guns blazing if I need you."

Kosugi thought for a moment and then nodded. He reached into his pocket and handed something to Jensen—a jade charm in the shape of a teardrop on a red string. It was the same charm that Jensen had found charred on his floor, a detail he had left out of the version he told Kosugi.

"What's this?" Jensen said, trying not to look like he just had all the wind knocked out of him.

"Something that's always brought me luck."

Jensen took the charm and slid it into his pocket. "Let's hope I won't need it."

There was a sudden commotion from inside the room. It sounded like a violent tussle. The noise startled Jensen and Kosugi. Shifty appeared unfazed.

A muffled voice cried out in pain from inside the room before being cut off by a horrible gasp and a series of choking sounds.

"Maybe we should come back another time," Kosugi said.

"Why?" Shifty replied like nothing had happened.

"Sounds like your man's got his hands full."

"I highly doubt that," Shifty smirked.

Kosugi made eyes at his partner, who responded by mouthing, *No turning back.*

Shifty knocked on the door once the noise inside subsided.

"Send him in," came a different voice that was equally muffled.

Jensen instantly recognized the room as being the room in the video. He saw the same furniture arranged in the same fashion. The same chocolate-skinned man with Master Po eyes was seated in a club chair wearing a cold expression. He had blood on his hands. Some on his face. A bloody butcher's knife lay on the coffee table in front of him.

Jensen noticed a pair of legs sticking out of the darkness on the floor beside the dealer's chair. The rest of the victim's body was hidden in darkness. Presumably the man they had heard crying out earlier.

Poor bastard.

Despite his apprehension, Jensen put on a brave face and continued over to the couch. He sat down, opened the briefcase, and slid it across the coffee table toward the dealer. Stacks of crisp, clean bills inside.

"You can count it if you want," he said.

The dealer closed the briefcase without looking at the money and pushed it away from him.

"Is there a problem?"

The dealer was slow to respond. "There are two kinds of people in this world," he said with the same quiet-cool menace that Jensen remembered from his nightmare. "Those who value immaterial things. Trust. Honor. Loyalty. And those who value money. Which one are you?"

Jensen pretended to think deeply.

"Think carefully now," the dealer added. "Your life

may depend on your answer."

Jensen tightened. *Tha fuck's that supposed to mean?*

"In so much as it relates to the decisions you make," he clarified.

Jensen's posture relaxed. He smirked at the power play, said, "I'd have to go with the former. What good is the money if you've gotta live your life looking over your shoulder." He looked over at the phantom legs sticking out of the darkness. "What'd this guy answer incorrectly?"

The dealer looked at the legs like the victim had slipped his mind.

"This man stood to benefit greatly from his deceit," he said. "So his punishment was equally great."

"What did he do? If you don't mind my asking."

The dealer leaned back in his chair and focused his weird, white irises on Jensen, said, "So, what can I do for you today, young man?"

I see.

"Well, I'm not gonna lie," Jensen said, turning on the spiel. "Wide Awake has been taking names on the street. It's making you a lot of enemies as a matter of fact."

Someone gasped in the darkness directly above the phantom legs, which then began to twitch.

"Excuse me a moment," the dealer smiled, and then he leaned forward, grabbed the bloody knife from the coffee table, and stabbed at the darkness several times, grunting with each downward thrust.

An agonized groan peaked with each savage blow. The phantom legs kicked, and then went still. Silence.

Afterward, the dealer calmly placed the knife back

on the coffee table, leaned back in his chair, and turned his piercing eyes on a semi-shocked Jensen.

"You were saying something about my enemies," the dealer said.

"I'm not one of 'em, by any means," Jensen assured, his heart slowly returning to its normal rate. "I'm not that stupid. I've been in the game long enough to spot a game-changer like your product. Everybody wants to get their hands on it. Or on you. And I mean everybody."

"Aren't you the least bit concerned that the rumors might be true?"

"What, that it's a government or alien conspiracy to control the population? Some shit about Biblical end-times," Jensen scoffed, although his current theory sounded equally implausible on paper. "Nah. I believe in facts and figures. And to cut right to it - I'm here because I want to be in the Wide Awake business."

The dealer continued to stare, unresponsive. Several uncomfortable seconds later, he smiled, nodded. "Good."

"I am curious about one thing," Jensen said. "You've only done business two other times this year, both following periods when Mercury was in retrograde. Being the curious kinda guy that I am, I did some research, and it turns out that from October 4th through October 25th—which was yesterday—Mercury was in retrograde. Coincidence?"

"What a strange question?" the dealer said, playing coy. "Have we met before?"

Jensen's expression turned serious. He repositioned his hand to allow for quicker access to his back-up weapon. Just in case.

"I think you know the answer to that."

The phantom legs twitched. The victim gasped awake.

Jensen used the distraction to go for his back up. The dealer's legs were briefly visible in his eye-line. There were hooves sticking out of the man's pants where his feet should have been.

Jensen made a funny sound, sat upright and laid eyes on a shrink-wrapped leather thing with Xs for eyes and a sphincter mouth sitting in the dealer's chair, wearing his clothing, and his unflappable swagger. This one looked older than the ones Jensen had glimpsed on the video, and it possessed an air of authority.

He blinked and the shrink-wrapped leather thing was gone, replaced by the dealer, sitting there as he had been all along.

"Please help me," the victim called out from the darkness in a voice that Jensen immediately recognized.

The victim leaned forward and into the light, validating Jensen's speculation that the phantom legs belonged to his partner.

But that's impossible!

Kosugi's hands were tied behind his back. His clothing was soaked in blood. His face was a map of bruises and ugly lacerations. But he was still barely alive, somehow.

Jensen went with his immediate reaction and snatched his gun from the holster.

"You son-of-a-BITCH!" he growled as he leapt to his feet and fixed his aim at the dealer's brow.

Out in the hallway, Kosugi sprung into action at the sound of his partner's outburst, drawing his gun, and shoving the shifty-looking man aside. He was momentarily stunned when the man hit the wall and shattered like glass.

Several gunshots rang out inside the room.

"JENSEN!" Kosugi called out as he rammed the door with his shoulder until it finally swung open.

He found Jensen inside, standing with his back to the door, in the middle of a giant pentagram painted on the floor in blood. The rest of the room was completely empty. Jensen's shoulders were slumped, his arms down by his sides. Plasma gun in his right hand.

Kosugi whipped his head around the room looking for someone or something to shoot. Finding nothing, he said to his partner, "You alright? I heard shots."

Jensen didn't say a word as he turned to face Kosugi. He had a blank look on his face. A single stream of blood leaked from his eyes, nose, and ears.

He locked eyes with Kosugi and lingered there for a moment. "We can't win this," he said. And then, without warning, Jensen lifted the gun to his head and pulled the trigger.

The blast popped his head like a meat-balloon.

Kosugi cried out, "Nooooo!"

2015 AD: The 64th Attempt

"So, explain to me what just happened?" the Asian teen said of the video-clip as he handed the cell phone back to the persistent brown-haired boy seated at the next desk over. The one who seemed way too eager to be his friend all of a sudden. He spoke quietly, eyes darting to the front of the room and back to make sure the teacher wasn't looking his way.

"You mean you don't remember any of it?" the boy responded. He sounded disappointed. Really disappointed.

"No. Why? What is it, some kind of found-footage movie or something?"

"Something like that," said brown-hair.

"Looks cool. Where'd you find it?"

"Somebody emailed it to me a couple days ago, along with a bunch of other stuff," the brown-haired boy said. "Really weird stuff. I've been reading through it over the past few days."

It was evident that the teen wanted nothing more to do with this weird, brown-haired kid, but the kid didn't seem to pick up on the cues. In fact, he leaned in closer to the teen and asked, "You didn't recognize the two guys? Or the dealer?"

"It was kinda hard to see on your phone," the annoyed teen replied. "I guess the dealer *did* kinda look like—"

"*Mister* Jensen and *Mister* Kosugi!" the annoyed teacher called out from the front of the room. "Maybe you two would like to share it with the rest of the class."

Danny Kosugi was pissed. He refused to acknowledge Jensen, who talked at him during the entire walk to the principal's office. Something about drugs, and leather demons, and time travel.

Kosugi had never been sent to the principal's office. In fact, he had never even been singled-out by a teacher for anything bad. He made a mental note never to speak to this Jensen kid again.

The boy virtually begged Kosugi not to go inside when they reached the office. He had to threaten the kid to make him stop.

Kosugi walked in with his posture on submissive and sat down in a chair ready to be admonished. Jensen was reluctant to enter, but finally did so. He was walking slowly, looking down at the floor.

His eyes crept upward and settled on the principal's waiting mug. He had a cold expression on his face, chocolate skin, and piercing white irises that no one seemed to find odd. The nameplate on his desk read: Principal Harbinger.

The principal smiled, said, "What's the matter, Mr. Jensen? You look like you've seen the Devil."

NIGHT OF THE
DAY OF THE
CELEBRATED
FOLKS

The man on the news kept talking about celebrities. Alan Mitchell had a thing about celebrity gossip contaminating his evening news.

"Vacuous chuckleheads," he'd grumble in response to reports on Bennifer one and two, Brittany's pregnancy, Brad and Jen, Brad and Angelina, and the like.

He hated that he even knew their names. He was ashamed to admit that he agreed with some of their politics.

Coming out of college, Alan's dream had been to find some forgotten little pocket of the country, settle down, and live off the land. So that's what he did, and for twenty-seven years he and his wife Irma enjoyed an almost utopian existence in Borden, Pennsylvania. Some hoity-toity magazine had even listed their tiny town as one of the best places to live in America.

At this very moment, the news was running footage of that comedian Carrot Top rampaging through the Shop and Save in Straussburg, which was no more than ten miles from Alan's place. Carrot Top was wielding a chainsaw. His face was covered in someone else's blood, and his large blue eyes stabbed through the terrifying mask.

The local news had broken into Alan's favorite show with the special report. *RED Alert!* was a reality show that focused on Detective Red Cypher, the cop who found the infamous tape that led to the demise of Hollywood culture. That made his a household name. Red was going to broadcast the tape that started it all on tonight's show.

Irma came walking out of the kitchen carrying a

sandwich—ham and cheese on white, no mayo—in one hand and a cold beer in the other. She set them down on the small, round table next to Alan's favorite chair and stood over him as he took a drink and swished it around his mouth.

"Just what the doctor ordered, hon," he smiled.

"Hope you can still afford my fee."

Irma gave her hips an exaggerated sway as she walked over to the large window next to the front door and peeked through the lace curtains. Alan watched her the whole time. After twenty-seven years, he still liked to lose himself in her beauty.

The *RED Alert!* theme music sneaked up on him. Alan whipped his head toward the television. The show was back on. And it looked like they hadn't shown the tape yet.

At the same time, he heard Irma clear her throat. "Ahhhh… honey…," she said.

"Yeah…" Alan replied from the side of his head. His eyes were glued to the television.

"Christopher Walken is outside."

***

VIDEO: UNMARKED POLICE CAR

We have rejoined *Red Alert!* during a silent intermission between colorful rants. The driver, Detective Red Cypher, taps his fingers on the steering wheel to a song that plays in his head. A cameraman films him from the backseat.

Cypher gives off the impression that he might become unhinged at any given moment, yet there is a playful confidence about him. The executives promote him as the rock 'n' roll detective. The name sticks.

Inner-city scenes flash through the windshield as Cypher drives. The bad elements give themselves away with suspicious stares that follow Cypher and his conspicuous car as it creeps past them.

CYPHER: (re: stares) Thaaaat's right... You *better* be scared. (To camera) I'll let you in on a little secret. You see that reaction? The way they all check themselves when I come rollin' through? I tell ya, that's what it's all about. Say you're having a bad day or something... You get that respect... that "yes Officer, no Officer" shit, and it lifts you right up. Makes you feel like pounding your chest or whipping your dick out or something.

CUT TO:

VIDEO: CYPHER'S OFFICE
The office is clean and orderly underneath the layer of clothing and paperwork. Framed pictures decorate the walls. From right to left: Muhammad Ali standing over Sonny Liston, a collage of comic-book covers, various photos of stunning graffiti murals, FOP commendations.

Cypher is sitting at his desk, framed by the large window behind him. He is holding up a VHS tape and letting it bounce to emphasize what he is saying.

CYPHER: Crazy world we live in. At no point in time has that been truer than right now. Just last week, I had to unload my gun into the women from *Desperate Housewives.* According to the witnesses at the Olive Garden restaurant, they went ballistic when the waitstaff treated them like "ordinary folk." "You can't talk to me like that! I'm famous!" That's what an eyewitness heard the small, dark-haired one say to her waiter while she was stabbing him. And unless you live on another planet, you're no doubt familiar with the brat pack massacre.

These are only a few examples on a long list that corroborates what I've said before, and what I'll say again: These people are not your friends. They do not care to about you. They thrive on your attention, your praise. Without it, they are powerless against you. But for those of you who still need convincing about their motives... or proof of what they can do, I give you Club Venus.

By now, you've all seen bits and pieces of the tape... heavily edited bits and pieces, I might add. This, however, is the first time that it's being shown to the public completely uncut. Oh... and if you have children... get 'em the hell away from the TV. This thing here ain't pretty.

CLUB VENUS (Eye-in-the-Sky surveillance footage)

August 23, 10:32 pm

A creeping stratosphere of funky barroom nicotine residue blankets the entire place, which consists of a large main room (bar, dancefloor, small stage up front, raised DJ booth) and a second floor loft that wraps around and looks down on it. The mood on each floor is vastly different from yet related to the other in that they both contribute to the painfully typical nightclub ambiance. In the main room, interesting-looking young and young-minded people are pressed chest to back from the rear of the place to the foot of the stage up front, squeezed shoulder to shoulder from the far right wall beneath the DJ booth all the way to the bar that runs along the far left side. They are waiting for something or someone. A banner hangs over the stage, partially obstructing the view of the large video screen built into the rear wall:

WFBB Presents: Brain Drain – *Lovin' 'em to Pieces* Listening Party

Upon the screen, a kinetic music video accompanies the passive-listening ambient melody. The music is laced with guitars and features a pulsating beat that sifts from speakers placed strategically throughout the building and is meant to satiate the crowd until the main event. It entices many within the crowd to sway slightly, while others simply stand facing the stage. Their faces gleam with anticipation.

The environment on the second floor is much more casual. There are people lounging on obnoxiously trendy furniture, leaning drunkenly against faux pillars, being observed by sculptures that have been welded and manipulated into pretentious designs. The people carry on quiet discussions spiked with innuendo— as quietly as they can manage without being totally drowned out by all the noise from downstairs.

A rainbow coalition of stagelights peers down into the crowd and up at the ceiling, passing through the blanket of smoke that gives them the appearance of ethereal density.

The crowd reacts to the portly, middle-aged man in a WFBB T-shirt who is working his way to the stage. His appearance (receding hairline, flashy tattoos, ponytail, circular shades) gives off the impression that he is trying hard to come off as younger than his years. They reach out and shout to him as if they know him.

The portly, middle-aged man jogs up the three steps onto the stage and walks out to the center, where a lone microphone stand awaits him, standing erect, its phallic head slanted downward. He wraps his meaty hand around the microphone and jostles it out of the U-shaped bracket. He looks at his watch, then over at the DJ. Sliding his hand across his neck like a dull blade, he signifies silence.

The music is the first to go, then the moving images on the screen, and finally the voices.

"Any of you kids come to hear some Brain Drain?" the portly, middle-aged man says playfully. The crowd roars with excitement. The portly middle-aged man looks momentarily annoyed at how long they take to settle down. He tries in vain to talk over them. He tries again.

A chant creeps to the forefront of the noise. "We want Brain Drain! We want Brain Drain! We want Brain Drain! We want Brain Drain!" The portly, middle-aged man rolls his eyes and signals to the DJ to start the record.

Silence…

The music starts. The portly middle-aged man walks off stage as the moving images resurrect themselves on the screen. Footage of Brain Drain's front man, Alistair Bane, rocking out, shirtless and sweaty, accompanies the music from the speakers. In the background, the other members of the band try their best not to look insignificant.

Gentle finger-flicks tickle guitar strings. The gloomy wail sounds distant, echoed. A slow thump, like a muddled heartbeat, creeps forward. The guitar chords sink into malevolence. A low organ bellow gives it meat.

Alistair begins the song in a whispering voice. His words are garbled by voices in the crowd (some of whom are singing along) and by the poor sound quality of the Eye-in-the-Sky surveillance equipment. The crowd is quickly entranced. They sway to the cadence of Alistair's voice, especially the ladies.

The music snowballs to an angry peak, Alistair's tone goes primal. The way he growls out the chorus sounds as if he's bearing his teeth and gums.

I don't care what the *fucking police* says!
Instead of fighting / gonna love 'em to pieces!
I don't care what the *federal beast* says!
Instead of fighting / gonna love 'em to pieces!

I don't care what that *hypocrite priest* says!
Instead of fighting / gonna love 'em to pieces!
I don't care what your *corporate release* says!
Instead of fighting / gonna love em' to pieces!

The chorus skips, and repeats. The DJ fumbles with his console to no avail. Something comes over the crowd. It happens suddenly. It's the looks on their faces—the ones we can see—and the deep swell in their chests as they began to breathe heavily. They turn to each other, fake joy illuminating their faces and pouring from their strained eyes. It affects everyone within earshot.

"I love you," people chant to those standing closest to them before lunging at them and exchanging deep, open-mouth kisses, teeth gnashing and lacerating gums, lips slipping and sliding on saliva and blood as heads dance with violent passion. They wriggle and writhe, arms snaking human contours, constantly reestablishing their aggressive embraces. "I love you, too," others reply.

Reacting with childlike glee to the feeling that has overcome them, they giggle and laugh and moan in euphoric delight. Speaking through emotional upheaval, they continue to turn to each other and chant. In a few of them, we can see terror hiding beneath the happy masks.

"I love you."

"I love you, too."

The crowd begins to strip naked, bare flesh shining through the dim atmosphere, the storm of sex vibes and the nicotine residue. Standing upright, they continue to embrace, limbs twisting around limbs, blind digits probing the warm spots.

Instead of fighting / gonna love 'em to pee-sez!
Instead of fighting / gonna love 'em to pee-sez!

The crowd's actions are becoming more and more aggressive, bordering on savage. Joyous sighs and orgasmic moans turn to screams laced with uncontrollable laughter.

Suddenly, it is everywhere. Blood.

"I love you," they say, as they lunge and bite down on their partners. Lips and tongues, fingers and breasts and erect penises are thrashed away with passionate savagery. Flesh and muscle rubber-snaps back to newly opened wounds that cough and spit blood and bile and strangely colored fluids.

"I love you, too," others respond through bloody backwash and in-between dumbed-down proclamations of agony. Bodies topple end over end from the second floor. Some are pushed or thrown. Some jump on their own, propelling themselves like weapons. Bodies litter the floor. Some lay completely still. Some twitch and scream and laugh, all at the same time.

Bottles, chairs, and uprooted fixtures are slung with full, brute strength. They crash down on unsuspecting skulls and shatter limbs. Knives and broken glass pierce soft flesh. Each doomed person goes out with a smile, laughing through the pain to deliver one last declaration of affection: "I love you."

Instead of fighting / gonna love 'em to pee-sez!

Instead of fighting / gonna love 'em to pee-sez!

Those still standing kick and stomp on the fallen. A bloody sheen covers the floor and causes many to slip and slide, yet they persevere. Three survivors stand ankle-deep in bodies and body parts, whirling in semi-consciousness. The tape skips. Wriggling interference steals away the picture and sound.

Club Venus (Eye-in-the-Sky surveillance footage) August 23, 11:10 pm

When the picture and sound return, the chorus leaps out at us in competition with the screams, the laughter, and the collision of solid objects and glass against bone wrapped in meat.

Instead of fighting / gonna love 'em to pee-sez!
Instead of fighting / gonna love 'em to pee-sez!

The three holdouts now lay dead on the floor. A group of horrified police officers wade cautiously through the devastation. "Somebody turn that shit off!" But before they reach the DJ booth, the music affects them too.

***

The inferno that destroyed Club Venus was officially ruled an arson. It was suspected that Sony Entertainment ordered the fire set to wipe out any evidence of the test. The Brain Drain listening party was picked at random to demonstrate the new, improved handhaber-technologie (manipulator technology) machine. The video feed was supposed to go directly to Sony, but a determined bootlegger who planned to post the unreleased song on the Internet hacked into it.

The technology was used by all levels of the industry—music, television, film, theatre—but there were only a select few who knew how it worked. Even knowing about it was a privilege of Hollywood's A-list, and most only knew tangentially of its existence. Rumor had it that the Third Reich supposedly developed the first machine in 1938 as a mind-control weapon to be used against Allied forces.

That machine went missing sometime in 1940 and didn't turn up again until fifteen years later, when Fritz Jansen, an assistant to Cecil B. DeMille, won it from a traveling merchant in game of poker. It was first used in 1956 on DeMille's production of *The Ten Commandments*.

The edited surveillance footage from Club Venus was first aired on FOX News after they mysteriously received a copy in the mail two weeks after the club burned to the ground. The package was marked "Burn, Hollywood, Burn."

In addition to side effects from the prolonged brainwashing, the doctors and scientists linked the technology to dementia, seizures, blindness, cancer, Alzheimer's, and obesity. The national news ran reports with titles like "The Slow Death of a Species" and "Hollywood's Dirty Little Secret."

The studios pulled out their big guns to fight what they were calling a witch hunt. With their money, they paid for new truths that implicated the conservatives, who they claimed to be behind this new smear campaign. It was most likely in retaliation for Hollywood's less-than-subtle stance on the war in Iraq and the Bush Administration in general, they said. They rolled out one blockbuster after another, bloated message-movies wrapped in formulaic packages aimed at swaying the public back into their corner.

All of them bombed.

The radio airwaves were overrun with ordinary people venting their scorn for Hollywood and equating the handhaber-technologie with Nazi experiments. *Mental euthanasia* became the buzz-phrase for what Hollywood had perpetuated on the public.

"I always knew they were up to something," one said.

"We should burn their city to the ground," said another.

Television sets were thrown out and/or destroyed by the hundreds of thousands. Movie theaters were burned to the ground.

Then came the attacks. Celebrities were targeted at random while shopping, dining at restaurants, or just driving down the street. There were shootings, stabbings, rapes, and beatings. Their homes were vandalized, sprayed with bullets and spiked with Molotov cocktails.

They got Madonna during her morning jog—ran her over with a tricked-out Escalade and kept on going. They found her by the side of the road, frozen in a triple-jointed, horizontal vogue pose. They got Paris Hilton too—stuffed explosives up her annoying little lapdog's ass. They got directors Uwe Boll and Paul W. S. Anderson—walked right up on them and beat them down. They got Jet Li and Yuen Woo Ping for all that wire-fu nonsense. Some old Chinese man named Lau Kar Lueng provided the angry mob with their addresses. They got Ryan Seacrest just for the hell of it. "Seacrest, out!" they shouted, as they stomped and kicked him.

It was becoming a game to people: 1000 points for superstars like Tom Cruise, Julia Roberts, and Oprah; 500 points for rock stars, rappers, boy-band flunkies, and all the boring pretty faces that infected UPN, FOX, and the WB; 100 points for recognizable character actors; and 50 points for has-beens. They even created a special category for celebrities deemed too annoying for words (i.e., ninety-five percent of contemporary hip-hop, R&B, or country music) and people who referred to themselves as divas or in the third person.

It got to the point where it was no longer safe for famous people to reside in places like Los Angeles and New York.

The news treated the mass exodus of celebrities as a monumental event in history. Along with a few reality shows, the news was the only thing left to watch on television, if you even had one anymore.

Aerial shots from helicopters revealed long lines of high-end automobiles, clogging streets and highways leading out of the big entertainment hubs. Famous faces hidden beneath inconspicuous clothing and thrown-together disguises crowded train stations and airports.

Fearing for their lives, a group of celebrities pooled

their money and created the "Celebrities are people, too" telethon to make the public understand that they were only pawns in a grand scheme. One after another, they pleaded in tears for the violence to stop.

For a while afterward, it did.

Many had lived too extravagantly after Hollywood's fall; as a result, their money dried up quickly. The bottom line was they needed jobs.

The integration of former celebrities into "normal work" was touch-and-go at best. There was still contempt for these formerly celebrated people. Now, they were working right alongside the very people who they had duped for decades in cubicle-filled office spaces, department stores, gas stations, fast-food restaurants, coffeehouses, etc.

Someone was always making trouble. Either people found fault with fallen stars' attitudes, which could come across as distant and arrogant, or they were smarting from being knocked off their regular-people pedestals within the workplace dynamic by honest-to-goodness beautiful people.

Some of the celebrities quit as a result. Others were laid off or fired for disrupting the workplace.

Jobless and unwanted, many of them took to the streets, panhandling, resorting to petty crime, and offering themselves to the highest bidder, sometimes just to stand in the background and look good. The smart ones formed the Union of Celebrated Individuals (UCI), a governing body to represent them as a collective.

The United States Government saw the UCI as a potentially dangerous nuisance, not far removed from terrorists. Meetings were held. It was decided that a national vote would be taken to determine their fate.

It wasn't long until the handhaber-technologie was mastered by the United States government. The military had used it to win the war with Iran. Instead of bombing the country, they hooked them on Hollywood. They hooked Pakistan, too. And they had their sights set on North Korea.

The new Middle East seemed like a logical place to send the celebrities. The White House leaned on the news media to push the "Iran Referendum" on the public.

It worked like a charm.

***

Thump! Thump! Thump!

The pounding at the door was growing more determined.

"This house… I like it. I think I'm going to have to take it off your hands," Christopher Walken said in his half-reserved, half-maniacal cadence. The heavy wooden door that was the only thing keeping him out muffled his voice.

"Irma, get your ass away from the window," Alan Mitchell hissed on his way down the stairs. He had gone up to the bedroom to retrieve his shotgun.

The news had interrupted Alan's favorite show again. Chaos leapt at him from the screen as footage from all over the country showed celebrities rioting in the streets. A disembodied voice spoke over the images.

"Members of the UCI have taken to rioting in the streets in protest of the unanimous vote to ship them off to settlements in the new Iran. Reports of celebrities commandeering suburban homes and estates are coming in from across the country. Authorities are urging residents to lock doors and windows. Do not attempt to engage the rioters. The National Guard has been deployed to deal with the situation."

"Hoooleee Sheeeyit!" Alan exclaimed. Although he knew about handhaber scandal and the rash of violence that followed, he hadn't turned on the television in the intervening weeks. None of that shit mattered to him way out here in Borden was how he felt. So why pay attention to it? *RED Alert!* hadn't been on in the last month while the vote and the media coverage that surrounded it was in full swing. When he first saw the footage of Carrot Top's meltdown, he figured it was an isolated incident. Just another celebrity with whom normalcy didn't agree.

The phone rang. Alan was standing right next to it. Though his reaction to it was involuntary—swatting down at it as if it were an insect—he managed to scoop it right up in his hand. He heard screaming coming from the receiver before he even lifted it to his ear. Instead of saying "hello," he just listened.

"Alan! Alan!" It was Jack Flannery, Alan's wimpy next-door neighbor. He sounded as if his life was in danger. "Alan! Somebody! Anybody... help us! Some actor just murdered my family with a fire ax. Elise, Marcy, little Jack Jr., they're all dead. I locked myself in the closet, Alan, but he's still got my fire ax and... Oh God, Alan... You've gotta help me! Please!"

In the background there was another voice, one that Alan immediately recognized from the movies.

"*SOME ACTOR?!* I have a name, goddammit! You hear me! I've worked with Pacino, Stallone, Schwartzenegger, Cruise, Oliver Stone, George Romero, John Singleton, and Denzel Washington, motherfucker. Rooker... Michael FUCK-ING Rooker. Who the hell have you worked with, huh? Joe What's-his-face over at the office? Now open that fucking door and get the hell outta *my* house, or so help me, I'll kill you too."

Thump! Thump! Thump!

"Maybe I wasn't clear before," Christopher Walken said into the door, "but this *house*... this *house* belongs to me, now. I'd suggest you pack up your things... and *leave* while I'm still in a decent mood."

Alan let the phone fall to his side. He could still hear Rooker yelling from the receiver as it rested on the floor.

Irma looked more terrified than he had ever seen her.

For a moment Alan just stood there, reeling from the footage, the phone call, and the uninvited guest at their front door. He took a deep breath and settled into his hunting mindset. He lifted the shotgun and pointed it at the door.

Panicked screaming poured from the television.

"Fucking celebrities, man! They're everywhere!" he heard a man yell into the camera.

"Oh my God! What's happening?!" a female voice screamed.

"*Well, it ain't the friggin' Oscars, folks,*" Alan

mumbled under his breath as he rested his cheek against the barrel, his finger curling around the trigger. "All right, honey. On the count of three, I want you to open the door and move out of the way as fast as you can."

Irma refused and cowered away, but Alan grabbed her by the wrist and stared with fury into her eyes until she overcame her fear and complied with his order. She slid her hand around the doorknob and nodded to Alan. She was trembling.

"Okay. Here we go. One... Two... THREE!"

Andre Duza is an actor, stuntman, screenwriter, and the author or co-author of over 10 novels, a graphic novel, Hollow-Eyed Mary, and the Star Trek comic book Outer Light, co-written with writer/producer Morgan Gendel. He has also contributed to several collections and anthologies, including Book of Lists: Horror, alongside the likes of Stephen King and Eli Roth.

Andre's distinctive blend of cult-horror, science-fiction, and dark comedy has been described as weird, off-beat, intense, horrific, satirical, and fast-paced, with a unique voice and lush, finely-detailed prose.

Andre also wrote, co-produced, and starred in the award-winning short film Tagati, which is currently making the rounds on the festival circuit. You can view the trailer on YouTube here: https://www.youtube.com/watch?v=uUZ6na3TBxI

deadite press

"Header" Edward Lee - In the dark backwoods, where law enforcement doesn't dare tread, there exists a special type of revenge. Something so awful that it is only whispered about. Something so terrible that few believe it is real. Stewart Cummings is a government agent whose life is going to Hell. His wife is ill and to pay for her medication he turns to bootlegging. But things will get much worse when bodies begin showing up in his sleepy small town. Victims of an act known only as "a Header."

"Punk Rock Ghost Story" David Agranoff - In the summer of 1982, legendary Indianapolis hardcore band, The Fuckers, became the victim of a mysterious tragedy. They returned home without their vocalist and the band disappeared. A single record sought by collectors, a band nearly forgotten, and an urban legend passed from punk to punk. What happened to The Fuckers on that tour? Why was their singer never seen again? No one has been able to say. Until now…

"Zombies and Shit" Carlton Mellick III - Twenty people wake to find themselves in a boarded-up building in the middle of the zombie wasteland. They soon discover they have been chosen as contestants on a popular reality show called Zombie Survival. Each contestant is given a backpack of supplies and a unique weapon. Their goal: be the first to make it through the zombie-plagued city to the pick-up zone alive. But because there's only one seat available on the helicopter, the contestants not only have to fight against the hordes of the living dead, they must also fight each other.

"The Book of a Thousand Sins" Wrath James White - Welcome to a world of Zombie nymphomaniacs, psychopathic deities, voodoo surgery, and murderous priests. Where mutilation sex clubs are in vogue and torture machines are sex toys. No one makes it out alive – not even God himself.
"If Wrath James White doesn't make you cringe, you must be riding in the wrong end of a hearse."
    -Jack Ketchum

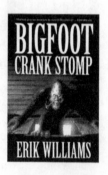

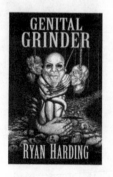

deadite press

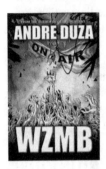

"WZMB" Andre Duza - It's the end of the world, but we're not going off the air! Martin Stone was a popular shock jock radio host before the zombie apocalypse. Then for six months the dead destroyed society. Humanity is now slowly rebuilding and Martin Stone is back to doing what he does best-taking to the airwaves. Host of the only radio show in this new world, he helps organize other survivors. But zombies aren't the only threat. There are others that thought humanity needed to end.

"Tribesmen" Adam Cesare - Thirty years ago, cynical sleazeball director Tito Bronze took a tiny cast and crew to a desolate island. His goal: to exploit the local tribes, spray some guts around, cash in on the gore-spattered 80s Italian cannibal craze. But the pissed-off spirits of the island had other ideas. And before long, guts were squirting behind the scenes, as well. While the camera kept rolling...

"Reincarnage" Ryan Harding and Jason Taverner - In the 80's a supernatural killer known as Agent Orange terrorized the United States. No matter how many times he was killed, he kept coming back to spread death and mayhem. With no other choice, the government walled off the small town, woods, and lake that Agent Orange used as his hunting ground. This seemed to contain the killer and his killing sprees ended. Or so the populace thought...

"Suffer the Flesh" Monica J. O'Rourke - Zoey always wished she was thinner. One day she meets a strange woman who informs her of an ultimate weight-loss program, and Zoey is quickly abducted off the streets of Manhattan and forced into this program. Zoey's enrolling whether she wants to or not. Held hostage with many other women, Zoey is forced into degrading acts of perversion for the amusement of her captors. ...

"Answers of Silence" Geoff Cooper - Deadite Press is proud to present the extremely sought after horror stories of Geoff Cooper. Collecting fifteen tales of the weird, the horrific, and the strange. Fans of Brian Keene, Jack Ketchum, and Bryan Smith won't want to miss this collection from one of the unsung masters of modern horror. You won't forget your visit to Geoff Cooper's dark and deranged world.

"Boot Boys of the Wolf Reich" David Agranoff - PIt is the summer of 1989 and they spend their days hanging out and having fun, and their nights fighting the local neo-Nazi gangs. Driven back and badly beaten, the local Nazi contingent finds the strangest of allies - The last survivor of a cult of Nazi werewolf assassins. An army of neo-Nazi werewolves are just what he needs. But first, they have some payback for all those meddling Anti-racist SHARPs...

"White Trash Gothic" Edward Lee - Luntville is not just some bumfuck town in the sticks. It is a place where the locals make extra cash by filming necro porn, a place where vigilantes practice a horrifying form of justice they call dead-dickin', a place haunted by the ghosts of serial killers, occult demons, and a monster called the Bighead. And as the writer attempts to make sense of the town and his connection to it, he will be challenged in ways that test the very limit of his sanity.

"Whargoul" Dave Brockie - It is a beast born in bullets and shrapnel, feeding off of pain, misery, and hard drugs. Cursed to wander the Earth without the hope of death, it is reborn again and again to spread the gospel of hate, abuse, and genocide. But what if it's not the only monster out there? What if there's something worse? From Dave Brockie, the twisted genius behind GWAR, comes a novel about the darkest days of the twentieth century.

AVAILABLE FROM AMAZON.COM

deadite press

"Brain Cheese Buffet" Edward Lee - collecting nine of Lee's most sought after tales of violence and body fluids. Featuring the Stoker nominated "Mr. Torso," the legendary gross-out piece "The Dritiphilist," the notorious "The McCrath Model SS40-C, Series S," and six more stories to test your gag reflex.

"Edward Lee's writing is fast and mean as a chain saw revved to full-tilt boogie."
- Jack Ketchum

"Ghoul" Brian Keene - There is something in the local cemetery that comes out at night. Something that is unearthing corpses and killing people. It's the summer of 1984 and Timmy and his friends are looking forward to no school, comic books, and adventure. But instead they will be fighting for their lives. The ghoul has smelled their blood and it is after them. But that's not the only monster they will face this summer . . . From award-winning horror master Brian Keene comes a novel of monsters, murder, and the loss of innocence.

"The Dark Ones" Bryan Smith - They are The Dark Ones. The name began as a self-deprecating joke, but it stuck and now it's a source of pride. They're the one who don't fit in. The misfits who drink and smoke too much and stay out all hours of the night. Everyone knows they're trouble. On the outskirts of Ransom, TN is an abandoned, boarded-up house. Something evil happened there long ago. The evil has been contained there ever since, locked down tight in the basement—until the night The Dark Ones set it free . . .

"His Pain" Wrath James White - Life is pain . . . . . . or at least it is for Jason. Born with a rare central nervous disorder, every sensation is pain. Every sound, scent, texture, flavor, even every breath, brings nothing but mind-numbing pain. Until the arrival of Yogi Arjunda of the Temple of Physical Enlightenment. He claims to be able to help Jason, to be able to give him a life of more than agony. But the treatment leaves Jason changed and he wants to share what he learned. He wants to share his pain . . . A novella of pain, pleasure, and transcendental splatter.

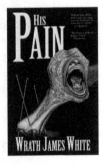

"The Haunter of the Threshold" Edward Lee - There is something very wrong with this backwater town. Suicide notes, magic gems, and haunted cabins await her. Plus the woods are filled with monsters, both human and otherworldly. And then there are the horrible tentacles . . . Soon Hazel is thrown into a battle for her life that will test her sanity and sex drive. The sequel to H.P. Lovecraft's The Haunter of the Dark is Edward Lee's most pornographic novel to date!

"Baby's First Book of Seriously Fucked-Up Shit" Robert Devereaux - From an orgy between God, Satan, Adam and Eve to beauty pageants for fetuses. From a giant human-absorbing tongue to a place where God is in the eyes of the psychopathic. This is a party at the furthest limits of human decency and cruelty. Robert Devereaux is your host but watch out, he's spiked the punch with drugs, sex, and dismemberment. Deadite Press is proud to present nine stories of the strange, the gross, and the just plain fucked up.

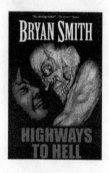

"Highways to Hell" Bryan Smith - The road to hell is paved with angels and demons. Brain worms and dead prostitutes. Serial killers and frustrated writers. Zombies and Rock 'n Roll. And once you start down this path, there is no going back. Collecting thirteen tales of shock and terror from Bryan Smith, Highways to Hell is a non-stop road-trip of cruelty, pain, and death. Grab a seat, Smith has such sights to show you.

"Apeshit" Carlton Mellick III - Friday the 13th meets Visitor Q. Six hipster teens go to a cabin in the woods inhabited by a deformed killer. An incredibly fucked-up parody of B-horror movies with a bizarro slant
"The new gold standard in unstoppable fetus-fucking kill-freakomania . . . Genuine all-meat hardcore horror meets unadulterated Bizarro brainwarp strangeness. The results are beyond jaw-dropping, and fill me with pure, unforgivable joy." - John Skipp

AVAILABLE FROM AMAZON.COM

CPSIA information can be obtained
at www.ICGtesting.com
Printed in the USA
BVHW041626310322
632882BV00007B/1022

9 781621 053071